DOUBLE-DECKER

More Tales from the John Radcliffe Bus

Edited by
Jackie Vickers

BOMBUS BOOKS
15 Henleys Lane, Drayton, OX14 4HU
www.bombusbooks.co.uk

DOUBLE-DECKER

All characters are fictional.
Although *Double-Decker* is based on many well-known places around Oxford any reference to living individuals is accidental

A catalogue record for this book is available from the British Library

ISBN 978-178456-426-1

First published 2016 by
BOMBUS BOOKS
an imprint of Fast-Print Publishing of Peterborough, England.
www.fast-print.net/bookshop

Contents

Acknowledgements v

The Authors vii

Introduction *Jackie Vickers* 1

Sandwich Cake *Anna Carr* 5

Home Truths *Karen Gray* 15

The Interview *Charlotte Ritchie* 23

Inspect the Unexpected *Jessica Woodward* 31

A Short History of Oxford *Rebecca Hotchen* 43

Trilby *Oliver Nesham* 53

The Guest *Pauline Massey* 61

Lucky in Love *Carol Macfie Lange* 67

Make Your Own Luck *Sarah Tipper* 73

Expecting *Anna Carr* 81

The Wrong Face *Jessica Woodward* 87

The Guilt Trip *Roger Marshall* 97

Rose *Pauline Massey* 107

Way to Go *Karen Gray* 113

No 13 Dreamcatcher *Charlotte Ritchie* 121

Chin Up *Pauline Massey* 127

The Untravelled Road *Rebecca Hotchen* 133

The Petrov Defence *Maria Mate* 143

After the Experiment *Jessica Woodward* 149

Cold Fresh Drinking Water *Karen Gray* 159

Everything I Do *Sarah Tipper* 171

Acknowledgements

This collection of short stories is a sequel to *Lucky 13*, published in 2015. Like the original book, it reveals the lives of passengers travelling on one particular journey of the No 13 bus which runs between Oxford Station and the John Radcliffe Hospital.

Once again, publication has been greatly assisted by the Oxford Bus Company and, in particular by Marta Skorupinska, who designed the cover and other graphics. *DOUBLE-DECKER* also has invaluable support from hospital charities: Oxford Radcliffe Hospitals Charitable Funds is using its resources to promote it among staff, patients and visitors, and the League of Friends in both the John Radcliffe Hospital and West Wing are selling it from their cafés.

Karen Gray has helped Jackie Vickers in making the text ready for publication. The writing competition on which this book is based, and the process of publication, was co-ordinated by Andrew Bax.

The Authors

Anna Carr is a midwife who lives and works in Oxfordshire. She studied at Oxford Brookes University and travelled regularly on the No 13 bus from Oxford Station to Jack Straw's Lane and the JR.

Karen Gray's first job was PA to the PRO of the BRMA. She soon escaped, and since then every job she has ever had has revolved around words and people. Happily, she is now free to keep up the good work and have some fun by writing fiction.

Rebecca Hotchen is an Oxford-based lexicographer who learnt the city first by bus and then by foot. She suspects the traditional next move is by punt.

Carol Macfie Lange is originally from Scotland. She now lives in the mountains of Andalucia, in Oxford, and in Albuquerque, New Mexico. She has published short stories and poetry and is in the process of finishing *Green on Snow*, sequel to her first novel *Invisible Child* about the disappearances during Franco's civil war in Spain.

Roger Marshall is a retired systems designer and company director who has lived just outside Oxford for ten years with his wife, Nina. After meeting in Kuwait they lived for 25 years in the Middle East. Active square dancers and bridge players, they have two grown-up children and two grandchildren.

Pauline Massey began writing stories in earnest when she was looking after a relative with Alzheimer's disease. She just had enough time to complete a story while her loved one was at a day centre for a few hours. She loves cats, travelling and disco dancing.

Maria Mate teaches German and English to adults for whom English is a foreign language; she also works as an interpreter, usually at the John Radcliffe Hospital where she helps patients from her native Hungary. Two volumes of her poetry have been published in Hungary.

Oliver Nesham spent most of his working life with books but took up writing only recently. He knows Oxford well and frequently uses the No 13 bus.

Charlotte Ritchie is a former Hansard reporter and researcher, who lives near the No13 bus route in Old Marston. When not walking her dog in the fields and meadows around Oxford, she is to be found Morris dancing with Cry Havoc Morris in Botley.

Sarah Tipper was born in Oxford and was very nearly called Robert. She mostly writes fiction about heavy metal music. She sometimes writes short stories about Christmas.

Jessica Woodward is a trainee librarian assistant and freelance translator. Having studied at Keble College and worked in the Corpus Christi, St Peter's and Taylor Institute libraries, she knows Oxford University well and enjoys using it as a setting for her stories. As well as writing, her hobbies include learning languages, going to Zumba classes, and obsessing over the novels of Jane Austen.

Introduction

JACKIE VICKERS

This collection of short stories arose from a request to provide a sequel to *Lucky 13* whose sale contributes to the Hidden Heroes Fund of the Oxford Radcliffe Hospitals Charitable Funds (registered charity 1057295). This fund supports staff recognition, development and training throughout the Oxford University Hospitals NHS Foundation Trust.

The original book was written by members of the Oxford Inc writing group. This time, however, it was decided to hold a short story competition, with the intention of discovering new talent. Short story collections are now more popular than ever as readers of fiction, pressed for time in their busy lives and finding novels too bulky and time-consuming, look for entertainment to be consumed at one sitting.

The stories in *DOUBLE-DECKER* are as varied as in *Lucky 13*. Characters can be as young as a pre-school child or the elderly who visit friends and family at the hospital. Their concerns vary from a student worried about the outcome of her interview, to the discomfort endured by visitors to a strange guest house. One struggles to defeat his anxiety, another with a lifetime feeling a failure; some tales depict sadness, others triumph.

All these disparate characters, as before, are linked by the No 13 bus which travels from Oxford Station to the John Radcliffe Hospital, past shops and colleges, flats and houses, providing both theme and structure to this book. Nor are the drivers forgotten, for we get an amusing glimpse into their interior lives.

We hope there is something for every reader in this collection that aims to entertain, but also to provide a snapshot of Oxford and its varied citizens.

oxford

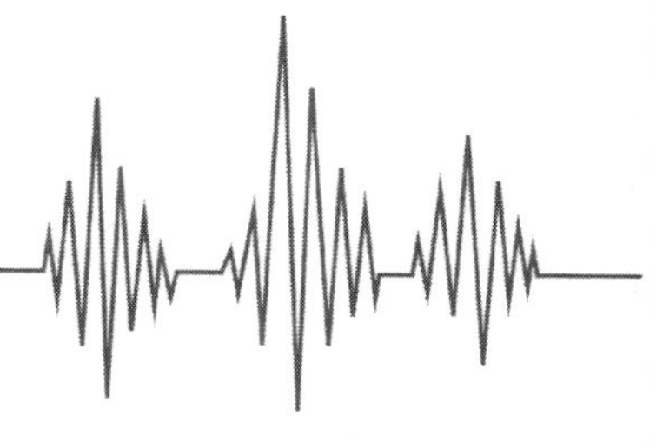

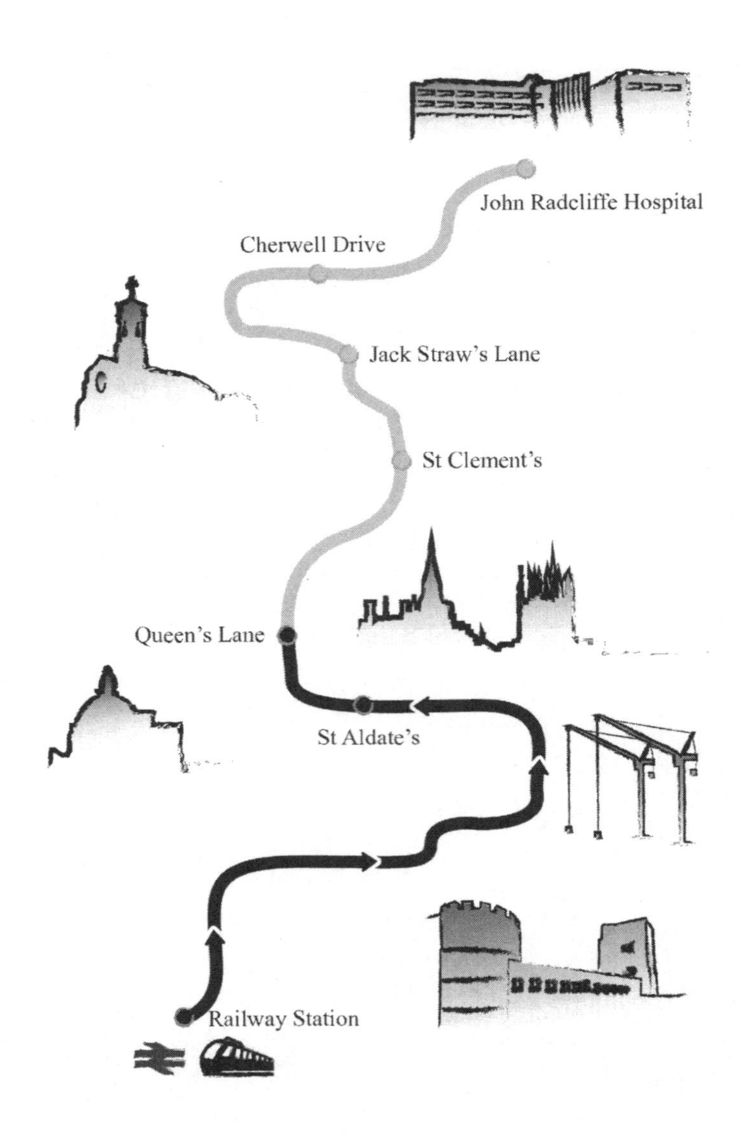
John Radcliffe Hospital
Cherwell Drive
Jack Straw's Lane
St Clement's
Queen's Lane
St Aldate's
Railway Station

Sandwich Cake

ANNA CARR

'Don't let her buy any more All Bran.'

The bus began to move as I typed the last word. My thumb slipped on the screen and the sentence changed to 'All Brain'. I frowned, corrected it and pressed the send button. The message departed with its little whooshing noise, away towards home.

I looked straight ahead, out of the front window. When had I last been upstairs on a bus? Perhaps when Milly was little. Pestering on a journey, the way little children do. 'Grandma, Grandma let's go on the top.'

It felt very high. The view slipped sideways as the bus turned. I tightened my hold on the metal bar in front of me. In my other hand, the phone buzzed with a return message from Jason. No words, just a question mark.

I typed again, concentrating on hitting the right letters in their tiny squares on the flat screen. 'She has enough to last her until Doomsday and anyway it disagrees with her tablets.'

An even quicker reply this time. 'Mum, not got time to go and see Nan today. Tell carer do shopping?'

For goodness sake. I bit down on my lip, hard. Swallowed the lump in my throat. One day, Jason. Please, just give me this one day. 'She needs visiting, even if you are too busy at work to take her shopping. She's on her own and all you need to do is drop in for ten minutes with an eclair and put her rubbish out.'

But who would have thought the old girl had so much life in her? She's still sitting up there like an outgrown dolly on a shelf, her head lolling forwards and her swollen legs dangling.

The mean-spirited, joyless old bitch.

Every bit as sour as one of the overboiled sprouts she infested every Christmas dinner with. At least she's too rickety to cook now, thank the Lord. That woman could ruin a roast dinner better than anyone I ever met. Beef like boot leather and flaccid Yorkshire puddings, then a tin of fruit salad and a splat of cheap vanilla soft scoop.

'Fantastic, Mum,' Ray would say, every time. She'd simper back and say, 'I know how you like things, dear.'

But every time she sat at my table she'd make some comment about the food. Something like, 'This is unusual, is it a new recipe?'

Then she'd poke at the lasagne or whatever, moving unacceptable contents to the side like a surgeon cutting out a cancer. Next she'd take a teeny nibble. Her lips would purse and her nose wrinkle then she'd put her knife and fork together and say, 'It's delicious, Sandra, but I'm just not very hungry today.' Then she would spend all afternoon dipping custard creams in the tea Ray made for her.

I remember the lasagne debacle because if I hadn't seen her tuck into a paving slab portion in a restaurant earlier that month I wouldn't have made it.

I was trying to be nice.

That would have been at least 20 years ago now, that chain restaurant. Somewhere near Norwich, a birthday. It might even have been Jason's 18th.

I can see him sitting at that table, looking out at us from under the long curtains of hair he had then. Was he drinking lager? No, Coke. Not 18 yet then. Still a child by the family rules of drinking, even with dinner. More like 25 years then. He's over 40 now.

How can I have a son that old?

Jamie opposite me - Coke and a steak. The old bag next to him, scoffing lasagne al forno like a starving timber wolf. Ray had fish and chips and I think I had something garlicky with chicken. Just the four of us, the whole family.

Happy birthday to someone.

Funny to think of Jason, with hair. He started losing it young and shaved it off before he was 30. That would be when he divorced energetic Emma and went off to find himself.

'Bugger finding himself,' Ray said to me. 'He wants to find a decent job.'

It's hard for the young ones though. Harder than it was for us. Jobs for life don't exist any more. Ray doesn't understand how it has changed. He left school, into the RAF then out of there and into a job with Redman's, just down the road from the base. There he stayed until he took early retirement. And me there all the time to move houses, arrange things, look after Jason and run about after Ray's old mum.

A group of teenagers shouted and joked on the pavement below me. All full of life and energy, running about while I sat still on a bus. I would have been a little older than them when I first saw this city, arriving at 17 for my nurse training at the Radcliffe. I looked out of the window again, searching for familiar things but seeing only how everything had changed.

When was I last here? Not for years.

Years and years.

The station was different too, with great big electronic barriers. Thank goodness it was quiet when I got there, I must have looked like a real old fool scrabbling about in my too-big handbag for my purse, then peering at the writing on the ticket over my glasses.

If the ghost of my young self was watching, she'd be mortified at what a fumbling, bumbling old biddy I'm turning into.

Can ghosts feel embarrassed?

They probably can't blush. Imagine it. Maybe you're staying somewhere nice, like that new hotel up by the Castle, the headless horseman comes galloping along a corridor and through the wall into your bedroom while you're getting dressed. 'Whoooooooo,' he says, then slaps a hand over the eyes of the head under his arm – 'Good grief, woman, put some pants on,' and turns red. Or whiter. More solid perhaps.

No, I don't think ghosts feel embarrassed. I think it's one of the things you leave behind when you move on. Emotions. Physical sensations. Pain. You're just a recurring image, like a film in someone's head.

That's the kind of thing I wonder, when I'm on my own. Like on that bus with no one to speak to, just watching and thinking.

'Do you want me to come with you, Grandma?' Milly asked me yesterday, while I was fretting about tickets and timings. She'd walked down to our house from her dad's. She's bored I think. Only just broken up for the holiday and she's bored already. She arrived on Saturday, all in black as usual with those mirrored sunglasses like the pilots wear. Tight leggings, black canvas boots and a top that shows her shoulders, all muscled from the rowing and swimming she does. She's like her mother. Energetic Emma was always doing something or other, I think that's why she and Jason got divorced. She left him behind. They got divorced ever so quickly, but then Energetic Emma did everything quickly.

She still does. I was at Jason's when she drove up in her shiny blue BMW and dropped Milly off. Poor kid was hardly in the door before Emma roared away, taking most of the gravel from the front drive in her spinning wheels.

You'd think she and Jason could at least speak to each other after all this time. I don't know why we were so upset when they split up, but we were. Even though Ray and I never liked Emma. Not really. We tried, but she so obviously thought I was just ignorant and silly. She used to look at me as if everything I said or did was beneath her contempt. She's tall - Milly takes after her - and back then she had all this springy dark hair which she wore put up with one of those big clip things. There were always bits trying to escape, flying off in all directions.

I'd say something and she'd look down at me, the hair bouncing round her face, and raise an eyebrow. Pause a moment before she spoke. Just long enough for me to catch her thinking *you stupid cow*. That's another one of those vivid films that plays in my head, again and again. Emma looking down at me.

We didn't want them to get married. Ray asked Jason, 'What do you want to do that for? You're so young.'

'I'm 22 Dad,' Jason said. 'Same age as you were when you and Mum got married.'

That was then, I wanted to say to him. *It was different then, that's what you did.*

That's what I did.

Everything was different. Oxford was different, when Joyce and I were student nurses here. Those endless hours ironing and tacking the seven pleats into the back of our starched caps. Terribly smart but completely impractical. One whiff of steam from the steriliser and the starch vanished, leaving you with a crumpled rag pinned to your head.

Joyce always managed to look smart, she never spilled things on her pinny or lost the starch from her cap. That's how you could tell us apart at a distance, the nurse tutors would say. We looked like each other, both short and dark and lively. But Joyce's energy went into her studies and her nursing. Her uniform crisp, her quick brain full of facts while my cap wilted and I forgot to do things. Joyce bailed me out all the time. In return I took her out into town, bought slices of Victoria sandwich cake in teashops and told her the facts of life.

Then she passed with flying colours, went to work in a hospital in London with her seven pleats in her cap and her spotless dresses.

And I married Ray, moved from base to base, had Jason. And now there's the grandchildren, Milly of course, and Jason's new little baby.

Ray's mother as well. She's always been difficult.

Joyce and I stayed in touch, once it had all blown over. We were too good friends to stay cross with each other for ever. At first just a few letters before she went to Canada. Then more recently email, Facebook, and now Skype. So she wouldn't be surprised that I got old. We'd seen each other on grainy, jumping video links across the sea.

It was difficult to get it set up. I sat in Jason's living room, looking at his computer, things dinged and beeped and he swore and clicked the mouse. Finally, pictures flickered into life and we got a sight of each other. Two old women peering into webcams. I looked at little old Joyce and I saw my face too in the window of your own video. We both looked so horrified I had to laugh. Then she laughed as well. We just gazed at each other and hooted with laughter, all the way from Cambridgeshire to Toronto.

Eventually, she wiped her eyes and said 'Hey, I'm coming to Oxford in April. We should meet up, catch up properly.'

'That sounds lovely,' I said. 'Why are you coming to Oxford?'

'It's a work thing,' she replied.

'Haven't you retired?' I asked. 'We're real OAPs now you know.'

'No rest for the wicked, Sandra,' Joyce said. 'You know that. As Sister Marsden used to say, if you've time to lean, you've time to clean.'

We laughed again, and chattered on for ages about all the old times and places, the nursing home and the tea shops of Oxford.

We'd promised to meet in April, so there I was. On the No 13 bus from the station, the route I'd researched on the Internet. Joyce said she'd spent ages on Tripadvisor looking for a cafe to meet in.

'We need cake,' she said while we were planning it. 'Really good cake and lots of tea.' Her accent is Canadian now, she said 'larts'. Larts of tea and cake. Different to the London accent she had when we lived in the nursing home together. Both of us grammar school girls, her from London and me from the sticks.

The streets looked so different from the top of a bus. A little knot of anxiety formed in my stomach. What if I didn't recognise the place to get off? Perhaps I should have stayed downstairs, asked the driver to tell me when we got to Queen's Lane.

I squeezed the cold metal bar again and took a deep breath. Then the bus stopped at some lights and I saw where I was. The corner onto St Aldate's, Christ Church Meadow straight ahead through the metal gates.

Another one of those memories played like a film in my head. Ray and I walking there, when we first met. Him, little and scrappy with his tattoos and the cigarette always hanging on his lip. Joyce, stiff as one of her own starched caps with disapproval when I got back to the nursing home, late and sunburned.

'He's a nice chap,' I said.

'Hmm,' she said, and went back to reading her book.

She came to our wedding, but she didn't want to be a bridesmaid. She said she didn't like the limelight but I knew it was because she didn't like Ray.

All these years later it was fine, as soon as we'd laughed at the old ladies on the webcam. We swapped stories. She told me about nursing in London, then all over the world. She finished up as a nurse tutor, as we used to call them. She waved a book at me in front of the camera, her name on the front. Edited by. Nursing for the 21st Century or something.

I showed her a picture of Ray. She said she didn't recognise him without his hair greased back and a cigarette in his mouth.

I looked down and shuffled through the photos I'd got ready in front of me.

'So,' I said. 'Anyway. This is my son Jason. He's really here.' I waved at him until he stood behind me and smirked at the webcam. 'And he's got the two children - Milly is nearly 17, and there's the baby as well.'

Joyce admired pictures, listened to stories, told me about her job, her apartment as she called it, her pets. She showed me some of the watercolour paintings she did in her spare time. Finally, she lifted up a plate, a piece of Victoria sandwich on it. 'I still use your recipe,' she said. 'I've told everyone, this is how you make a proper sandwich cake.'

'So Jason's been married twice?' She asked. 'The energetic one, yes? And then…?'

'Fiona,' I said. I tried to keep my voice light, but Joyce noticed. I saw her head tilt and her eyebrow raise, the way it always had. The way it had when I'd told her I was going to marry Ray and not be a nurse after all.

'Yes, Fiona.' I said again. 'She's very nice. She works hard at her business and she needs some time to unwind as well so I look after baby Dexter four days a week.'

'Oh my,' said Joyce. 'You're a sandwich carer.'

I laughed again. 'What does that mean? I look after the egg and cress?'

'No,' she was smiling but frowning at the same time. 'It means you look after the older generation and the younger ones too.'

'Well, someone has to,' I said. 'Jamie and Fiona have to go to work, and Ray's mum is very frail these days.'

'When do you get time for yourself?' Joyce asked me.

'Oh,' I said. 'I do the crossword, you know. I enjoy having Dexter around, he keeps me young,' but my voice sounded tired and I looked again at the old woman on the webcam, the pouchy eyes and the slack skin. Grey hair needing a good cut and glasses slightly wonky ever since Dex grabbed them and pulled the arms apart.

'April,' said Joyce. 'Larts of tea and cake. My treat.'

'Yes,' I said. For some reason I had a lump in my throat and my eyes were full of tears.

The bus reached the top of St Aldate's. Carfax Tower. The High Street. My phone buzzed again. Fiona, this time. 'I need u 2 have Dex 2morrow got a mtg @11.'

Between that and Ray's mum's hospital appointment that would take care of the day.

So much for the crossword.

I stood up as the bus crept along the sunlit street, past the pale stone colleges and the smart shops. Carefully down the stairs, hanging on tight to the bannisters then off the bus and into the moving crowd. All the people with their stories walking along the pavement. All the phones ringing and messages whooshing around the world.

I stood still a moment, looking. Ahead of me I recognised the cafe Joyce had found, and outside it an old woman with a hiking stick and a handbag as big as my own. I looked past her, confused, half looking for the Joyce I'd known, the quick, vivid girl with her huge smile. Then I saw her in the old woman. The same smile, the same quick wave. Just for a second, the sun shining on her white hair made it look like an old fashioned nurse's cap.

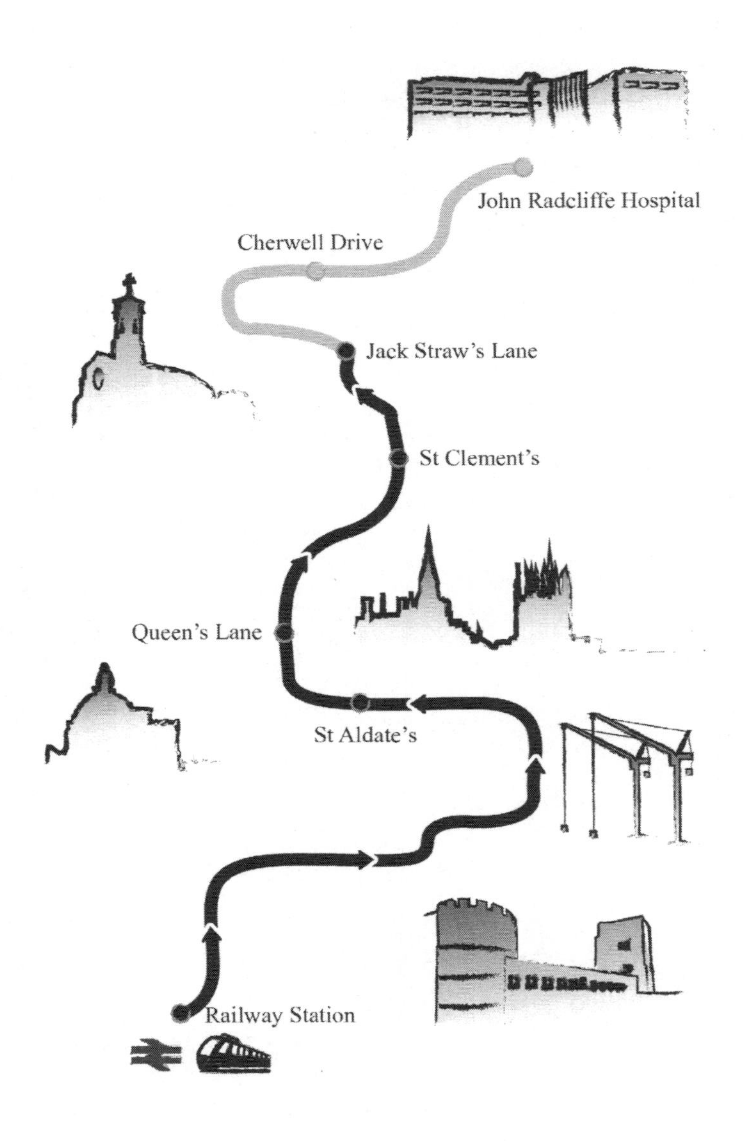
John Radcliffe Hospital
Cherwell Drive
Jack Straw's Lane
St Clement's
Queen's Lane
St Aldate's
Railway Station

Home Truths

KAREN GRAY

The question puzzles Ellie. She tops and looks at her mother. What sort of a question is that? Her tall, kindly mother is always ready to hear about Ellie's day. She listens quietly without interrupting, her head on one side, hair tucked behind her ear. Sometimes there is a pause while she thinks about what she has heard, then they will talk about it. She does ask questions sometimes, but she has never asked one like this before.

As they walk along the street together, Ellie can tell that her mother is waiting for an answer and will say nothing more until she has one. Ellie thinks for a moment, decides, gives the answer she knows her mother wants to hear and goes back to hopping and jumping along the pavement, bunches bouncing as she counts how far she can get before landing on a crack between the paving stones.

Ellie and her mother take the No 13 bus to Nana's house every Tuesday and Thursday during the school holidays. They do this so often that some of the bus drivers recognise them and smile at Ellie. She always smiles back politely. They get off the bus at Marston and walk to Nana's house, then Ellie's mum goes off to work at the hospital and leaves the bright-eyed little girl and the smartly dressed, grey-haired lady to amuse each other, knowing how much they look forward to their time together. These days are a gift to the three of them.

Today is no different. Nana takes Ellie's coat while her mother bends to hug her saying,

'Be a good girl for your Nana.'

Ellie frowns. *I am me,* she thinks, *I can only be me.* Outside again on her way back to the bus stop, Ellie's mum looks back at the house. Inside, Nana takes Ellie's hand and they both wave through the window with their free, outside hands, like two of the concertina dolls they sometimes make together, cut out from folded paper.

Ellie and Nana do a lot of cooking on Tuesdays and Thursdays. Her grandmother has noticed how Ellie watches and learns everything, observing from a distance, and then practising the new skill until she masters it. They have moved from making fairy cakes (Ellie is very good at licking the bowl, carefully scraping up every last trace of cake mixture with her favourite spatula), to their best creation yet, the gingerbread house which was Ellie's surprise present to her parents last Christmas. Nana remembers how carefully the little girl had placed overlapping chocolate buttons one by one on the roof of the house until it was completely covered, the rows ruler straight, with exactly the right number of buttons in each row although she didn't seem to be counting. Ellie learns things that her Nana doesn't show her. Nana learns too. Like the day they went to have coffee and juice with the next door neighbour and her young family. Ellie was staring at the hutch on the grass.

'Look, there's a mouse!'

'No, it's a hamster.'

'It's a mouse, Nana!'

'No, Ellie, mice have tails.'

'No they don't, look!'

Sometimes they pick peas from Nana's garden. Once back in the kitchen, they set to work. Two heads bowed over the colander in concentration, Ellie on the pea pods, her grandmother on Ellie. The elderly woman kisses the top of the little girl's head. Ellie doesn't notice. She picks up a chubby, promising peapod and presses on the rounded end as she has been shown, the end where the flower was, not the end with the stalk. She presses till it pops open then splits the pod down one side to make a chute. Next she urges the brilliant green peas down the chute with her thumb until they rattle into the saucepan. Pop. Push. Rattle. Pop, push, rattle. When all the pods are empty, Nana takes the pan with the peas to the hob and says,

'We'll have these for our tea, shall we, Ellie?'

'No thanks, Nana, I like your usual peas from the freezer best.'

The day is breezy but sunny, spring flowers brighten the ground under the trees outside. When they get to the park, Ellie runs off to pick daisies while her grandmother settles down on a bench by the side of the path.

'Give me your doll, Ellie, she can sit here with me!'

She tucks their snack bag under the seat where she can feel it safe on the ground against her leg. A bottle of water for Ellie, flask of tea for herself. Rice cakes and raisins for them to nibble on. Pity about the KitKats she had bought the day before, but the frown on her daughter's face earlier when she saw them was warning enough; they were quickly put away in the cupboard out of sight. Never mind, she would enjoy one on her own tonight as she watched the News at Ten before bed. They would have stayed nice and cool in the new, insulated bag.

Ellie brings handfuls of daisies back to the bench and sits down. The stalks are all different lengths, some far too short for daisy chain purposes.

'Will you help me make the holes, Nana?'

They set to work, one set of fingers, stiffer than they used to be, holding the daisy stalks and splitting the stem just above the end with a frosted pink thumbnail. The smaller, nimbler fingers gently thread the daisies through one hole after another to make a string.

'That's enough, Nana!'

'Not yet, Ellie, we have to make it long enough to fit over your head.'

'How do we join it up to make a necklace?'

'Ah, that's the tricky bit. We have to push the whole head of the first daisy through the split in the stalk of the last one.

I'll show you, but your little fingers might make a better job of it than mine.' Ellie nods. They smile at each other and carry on splitting and threading.

'Nana?'

'Yes, Ellie?'

'Do you always have to tell the truth, absolutely always?'

'Well yes, I would say so. Isn't that what Mummy and Daddy say?'

Ellie picks up a daisy stem which is split right to the end. She throws it on the ground. 'Yes. But what if you can't?'

'I don't understand, Ellie.'

'Yesterday they asked me the same funny question, but not at the same time.'

Nana stopped splitting. She was all attention but she tried not to show it. 'And what did you answer?'

'I told them both the same thing.'

'What was that?'

'I said, *with you*, but that's not possible. Nana, does that make me a bad girl?"

Nana felt the prickle of tears at the back of her eyes.

After they have wriggled the necklace safely over the little girl's head and past the bunches, Nana sits and thinks and watches as, one by one, Ellie slowly pulls the petals off the daisies they had rejected because their stalks were too short to be part of the necklace. The little girl's lips are moving as the petals fall onto her lap.

'Are you playing *he loves me, he loves me not,* Ellie?'

'No, Nana, not that one.'

From her bedroom, Ellie can hear her parents' voices thrumming through the floor and up the stairs. That, or the radio in the kitchen, are the usual soundtrack to playing in her room with her doll after lunch. The familiar sounds of home. But lately, the voices have changed their tune. Ellie listens as she kneels on the floor and undoes the buttons of Dolly's dress. The little pink and purple case where the doll's clothes are kept is open on the floor beside her, yesterday's daisy chain droops on the knob of the white bedside table where her mother had hung it the evening before. Ellie can't hear what her parents are saying but the muffled voices are getting louder, insistent, disturbing. Is somebody being told off? She hugs Dolly to her chest,

'It's alright, Dilly Dolly, don't worry, I'll take care of you.'

In a moment, the voices get softer again, they seem further away and Ellie realises that her parents have moved out into the garden at the back of the house. She gets up to look out of the window and sees them both, her mother is sitting at the wooden table with her arms wrapped round herself, rocking slightly. Her father is pacing up and down, his mobile phone in his hand, jacket on the back of a garden chair. Ellie turns away from the window, does up Dolly's buttons again and picks up the little suitcase.

When the policemen have drained their mugs of tea, put away their notebooks and gone, three dazed adults sit round the kitchen table, trying to take in the events of the last few hours. Ellie is on her mother's knee, tidying Dolly's tangled hair.

The two policemen had recapped Ellie's story, smiling as they did. Not all their call-outs ended as quickly or as well as this one, but there were no returning smiles from the listening adults as they heard how Ellie and Dolly had set off on their usual route from home to the No 13 bus stop. Just as they got to the waiting queue of people, there was a sudden fuss over a lady who had fallen down chasing her hat when a gust of wind blew it away. Everyone was either busy helping her or watching the goings-on. Ellie realised that she didn't have any money to pay for her ticket, so when the big red bus rolled up, Ellie tagged along behind another, older lady with a shopping bag who had been standing in the queue, watching. The lady seemed very glad to get to her seat on the bus and made an *Ooof* sound when she sat down. She was holding a flowery pink walking stick which made her look very friendly. Ellie had given an excellent description of the lady, one policemen said. Ellie found a seat behind everyone else at the back of the bus and when the bus reached the Marston stop, she got off with a young couple who had funny coloured hair. The driver stared at them when they walked past him and didn't look at Ellie. The girl's hair was bright pink at the front. Ellie thought that was fine, but she didn't like the boy's blue hair so much. Walking to Nana's house was easy. She hadn't expected Nana to be out but decided it didn't matter, she and Dolly would just sit and wait on the doorstep until she came back.

That was exactly where the policemen found them when they drew up in their car. Ellie's parents had reported her missing having got no reply from her grandmother's home phone or her mobile. They rang the police and gave them the address before her father grabbed his car keys to drive round the streets in a panicky search for his lost little girl. Nana had arrived home from the Oxford Central Library to find quite a crowd on the doorstep.

'What made you come on the bus here to Nana's all by yourself, Ellie?'

Her father breaks the silence as he strokes the little girl's head, the other hand on his wife's shoulder. She looks up at him, still trembling, and hugs her daughter a little too tightly, unable to suppress the painful stabs of memory: calling up the stairs for Ellie, the echoing stillness, the shock of the empty bedroom.

Ellie's head is down, her bunches droop past her chin.

'I made you and Mummy cross.'

'Why did you think that was your fault?' Her father's voice sounds gentle. His hand rests on her head.

'Because I didn't tell you the truth.'

There is a pause. Ellie's grandmother sits very still, only her hand moves as she fingers the pendant round her neck. Its blue-green stone gleams in the wan April sunshine edging through the kitchen window. Her daughter and son-in-law glance at her. She nods.

'You mean, when we asked you who you would rather live with, Ellie, Mummy or Daddy?'

It's the little girl's turn to nod. She bends over Dolly. Her father drops to his knees and throws his arms round the three of them.

'Now, I'm going to ask a question.' Nana gets up and reaches for the cupboard door.

'Who wants a KitKat?'

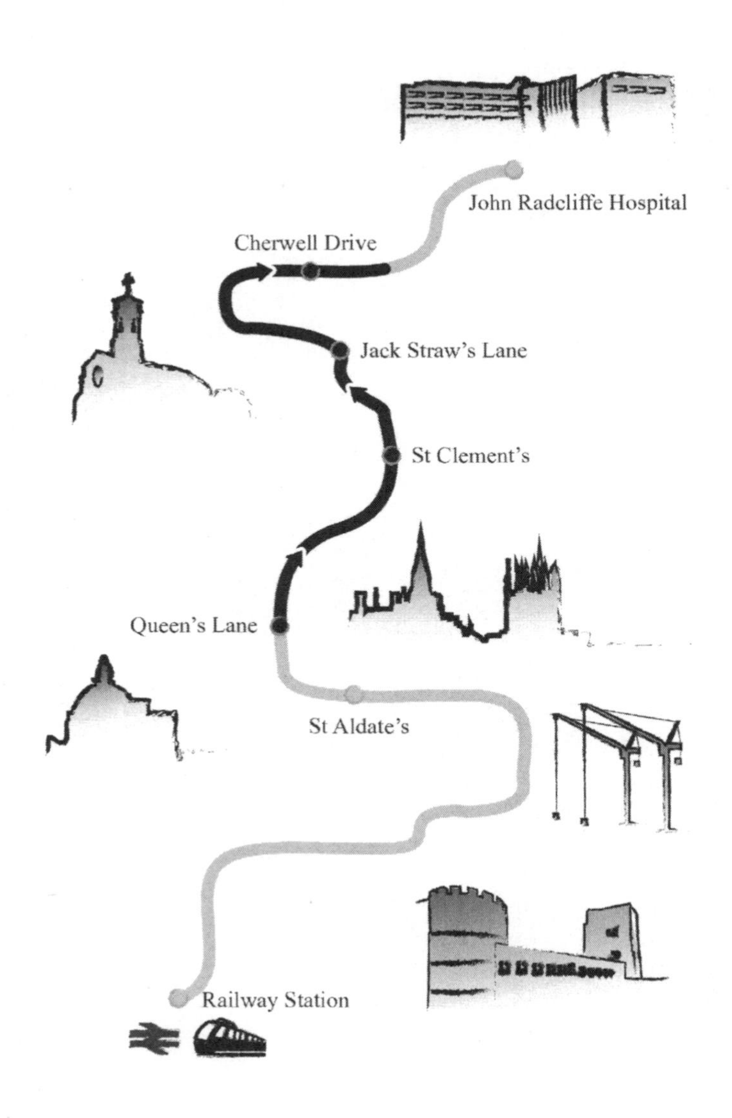
John Radcliffe Hospital
Cherwell Drive
Jack Straw's Lane
St Clement's
Queen's Lane
St Aldate's
Railway Station

The Interview

CHARLOTTE RITCHE

She waited at the No.13 bus stop at Queen's Lane. Earlier that morning the No 13 had carried her, and her hopes and dreams, serenely along the Marston Road. She had waved her father goodbye, and boarded the long low red bus. She was excited, nervous and unsure of which stop she wanted. The driver smiled as she said,

'Do you stop near University College?'

'We certainly do. I'll give you a call when we get to that stop.'

And she'd settled down, almost relaxed, in the warmth and comfort of its seats. That had been six hours earlier, when everything had seemed possible.

Now, six hours later, she waited in The High for the No 13 again. She wanted the bus to come, to take her away from this city centre with its smug shops and college walls. She was sick of it all; the posh accents, the traditions, the ridiculous gowns and black and white, and most of all, ambition. She fought back the urge to cry as tears welled up. She had allowed herself to think for just one moment of home. Her lovely, lovely home, tucked quietly into the lee of the hill above Reeth in the Yorkshire Dales; the only sound the sheep, the curlew and the occasional farm dog. She could imagine her Mum, even now, wandering down the lane to the post box, waving one hand in the air as she tried to find a signal for her mobile phone.

Oxford, the city of her dreams, had become her nightmare. She had worked so hard to get here, had applied to one of its most prestigious colleges, and had made a fool of herself. Twenty-four hours ago, she had been excited. Nervous, yes, but excited. She had rehearsed for the interview with her Mum every evening for a fortnight, and had revised everything she knew, and some things she didn't know, about history, and it had all been in vain. That very morning she'd taken the No 13 up The High, dreaming of being a student at University College, and now it was all in tatters. The interview had started badly. She'd never been in such austere surroundings, surrounded by so many southern accents or smartly dressed students. She'd knocked on the door, and upon entering seen an elderly man sitting comfortably in an armchair. Next to him, on a table, were some objects. She noticed a sword, a ration book, a Suffragette poster, and a photograph of Gandhi, but had scarcely considered their purpose before he struck. Leaning forward, his gaunt face scarcely relaxing into a smile, he picked up a black and white postcard of people from long ago, perhaps the 1920s, dressed in pantomime costumes, with one of them dressed as a knight. She turned it over. The print identified it as somewhere called Bacup.

'What can you tell me about that?' he'd asked.

She looked at him. What did he want to know?

'It's in Lancashire', she began. She knew Bacup well. Her grandfather had been a train driver, and she'd been brought up on the history of the line.

'I'm not sure what the people are doing,' she began, 'but Bacup symbolises all that is wrong with the UK today.'

What had come over her? She had told herself time and again not to give her opinions. She was a keen member of the Green Party, and was passionate about public transport.

The Don leaned towards her.

'I was more interested in the Mumming Play you see there,' he said, his eyes glinting slyly.

Now she remembered. Yes of course. Bacup had a tradition of performing Mumming plays. She'd seen one; all about St George.

'The trouble with Mumming plays,' she began, 'is that they retell stories of old. They do add modern bits in, which can be interesting, but essentially they are repeating history rather than making it.'

She'd felt rather pleased with this last rejoinder, but the Don had only leaned further forward, his yellowing teeth sharp as a wolf's.

'And what is so important about the train line?' he'd asked.

Where should she start? She had tried to explain how important the line had been to the wool and slipper industry. How silly it had sounded. She had remembered the date - 1966 - when the last train to Bacup had run its final journey. A hiss of steam, her grandfather had said. In her mind she heard the train doors slam on that hot summer's day, just as her grandfather had told her. She saw the porter walking briskly down the platform, pushing his trolley, and she smelt the warmth of the carriages with their thick upholstery.

She described all that she knew about the Rossendale Valley, with its dark valley floor where the train line ran, and its wonderful uplands with the farms and distant factory chimneys.

The Don was sitting back now, with his eyes almost closed. She was boring him. She stopped.

'Sorry', she said.

'Can you tell me why that train line was important and why you feel it important now?' he asked.

'It was important then,' she'd said, 'because local industry depended on it to bring in the raw wool and coal, and to take away the finished products. But more than this – it was a line of communication.'

He looked faintly annoyed.

'The train and its passengers brought news from Rochdale and other places. It linked us in to the rest of the country. That's why it was important,' she added rather lamely.

'Is that it?' he sneered.

'No,' she'd added, feeling her high horse approaching and knowing that she was unable to stop it. 'If we could get that line, and so many other lines reopened, it would bring the North alive again. It's a clean and sustainable form of transport. Bacup is an economically depressed area. We could bring it alive again.' She'd faltered. Her horse had stopped quite suddenly.

The Don opened his eyes.

'Thank you Miss Ford. We'll be in touch.'

She had mumbled a 'thank you', and walked out, mortified. To think that all her knowledge about the Reformation, Victorian England and two world wars had ended like this. She stepped through the college door and out onto The High. Across the road, people were queuing for their buses. Her father would be waiting for her, in the little cafe in Cherwell Drive, where he'd conveniently managed to arrange a meeting with an old friend.

She leant back against the wall of All Souls and fought back tears. She'd worked so hard. Another squall blew down The High, and behind it the now welcome sight of the red No 13. A small group of people started to be drawn towards the No 13 bus stop. She joined them, enjoying the normality of it all. She was back amongst people, ordinary people. The bus was almost full, and she glanced quickly round, estimating the sizes and faces of the passengers, before making a quick choice, and sitting herself down next to a young man, about her age, who shifted uneasily towards the window to let her take her place. She opened her bag, trying to find a tissue. Instead she found the letter from University College, inviting her to attend for an interview. She ripped it up, and began to stuff the pieces into her coat pocket. The young man glanced at her.

'Didn't go too well then,' he said, his eyes friendly and warm.

'No. I had an interview and made a complete fool of myself.'

He smiled and pointed out Magdalene College as the bus sped over the lights, heading for the bridge.

'That's my college. I hope you do get in. Lots of people hate the interview, especially if you're from up North and feel a bit out of place with all the southern accents.'

She knew he was trying to be kind.

'It wasn't just that,' she began.

'What was it then?'

'Just everything. It's so different from my school but everyone else seemed at home. And then the tutor interviewing me – well, I've never met anyone like him before.'

The young man smiled.

'Yes, they can be a bit odd at first,' he said.

'I love it here,' he added. He looked across at her. She was still trying not to cry.

'I'm doing medicine,' he said. He nodded towards the open road ahead.

'I'm shadowing doctors up at the JR. Not everyone's cup of tea, but I like it.'

She looked out of the window, still desperately holding back the tears that she knew would come as soon as she saw her father.

'Will you come if you get offered a place and get the grades?' the young man asked.

'I would have done,' she said, trying to smile, 'but I haven't a chance now.'

The bus was approaching the parade of shops at Cherwell Drive. Her heart began to sing; her father would be there. She pressed the button to stop and began to assemble her things, ready to get off.

'Well, look me up if you make it,' he said. 'I'm Dave Smalley. At Magdelene. I'd be happy to show you round.'

She thanked him and began to walk towards the open door of the bus.

'Bye then,' he said.

'Bye Dave,' she replied.

Then her heart leapt. There he was; her father. Ill-fitting suit and slightly battered briefcase, standing just by the bus stop. He was smiling the smile that says, 'You're home now girl, so don't you worry.'

She flung her arms around him and buried her face in his chest.

'That bad?' her father asked.

She nodded, the tears now streaming down into his slightly crumpled shirt.

'Never you mind,' her father said.

'We'll be home in no time and you can forget all about it.'

As they walked towards their rather battered Ford Focus, the Don scribbled 'accept' on her form. He leant back in his chair. Yes, that one would go far. She had brains and guts and a lively and inquiring mind. Just what University College was looking for.

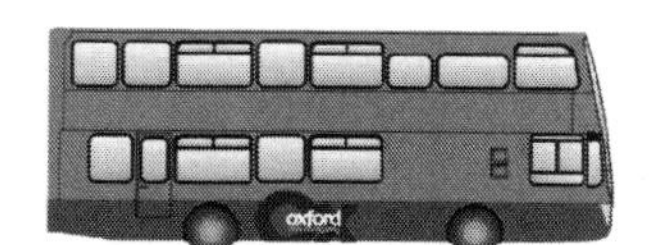
oxford

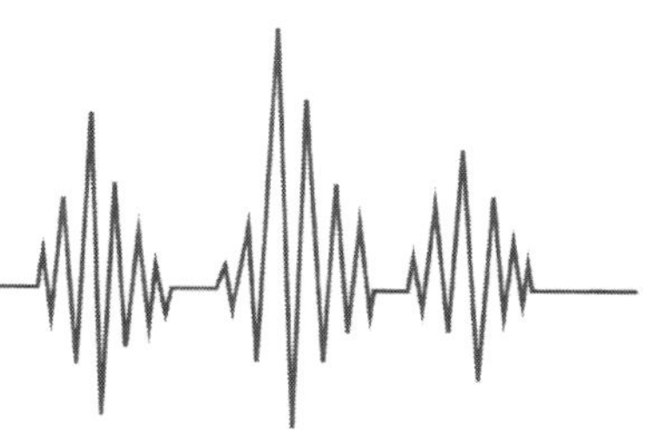

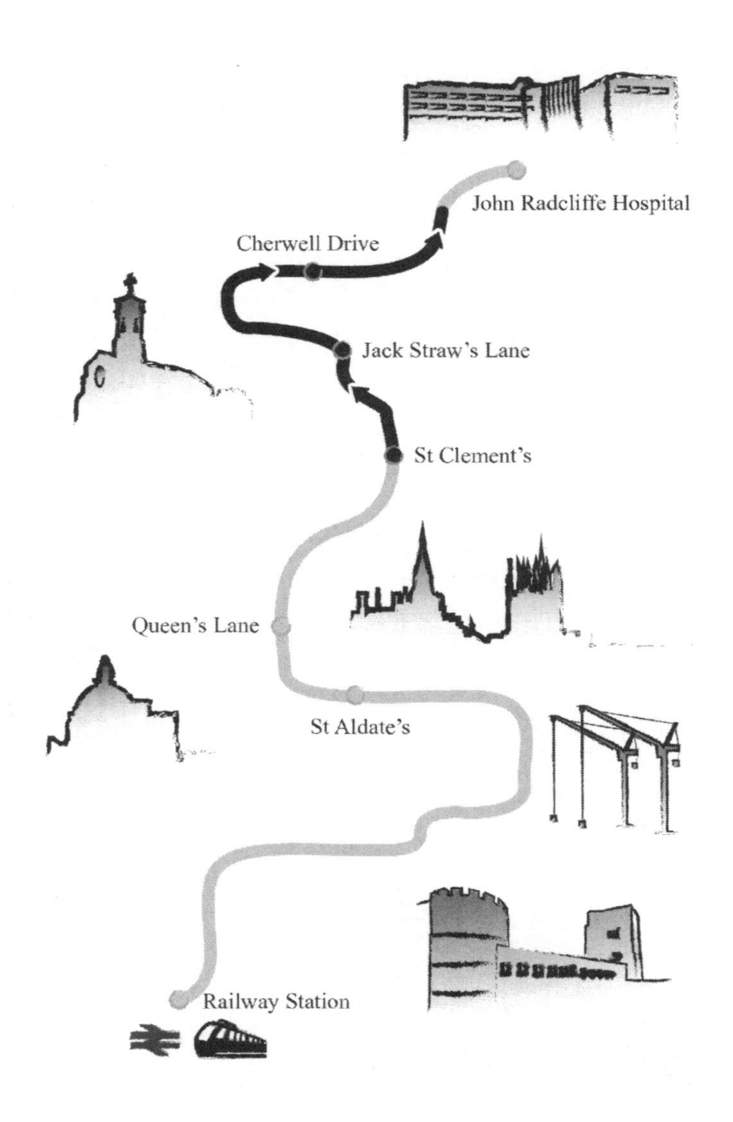
John Radcliffe Hospital
Cherwell Drive
Jack Straw's Lane
St Clement's
Queen's Lane
St Aldate's
Railway Station

Inspect the Unexpected

JESSICA WOODWARD

If you leave the bus in mid-St Clement's, take a few wrong turns and a walk on the lonely side, you might find yourself face-to-face with the home of the Grots.

Or, at least, it *was* simply a home until they came into an unexpected and mysterious fortune and decided to realise Mrs Grot's long-standing dream of running a hotel.

Lychees Hotel is a boutique establishment, fronted by a yard filled with whichever species of potted plant Mrs Grot believes is in fashion at the moment, and backed by a little conservatory that the brochure describes as 'The Sunshine Bistro'. The brochure will also tell you that in the Sunshine Bistro you can enjoy a select range of British delicacies, that in the Relaxation Lounge unique Entertainment Nights are held, and that throughout the length of your stay, you can expect frequent and attentive room service.

If you have lingered long enough to take a brochure from the plastic box fixed to the gate and absorb all of these details, you will probably find that Mrs Grot has appeared at one of the windows to size you up. Mrs Grot prides herself on her psychological insights. She will discover plenty to feed her running commentary to Mr Grot – who will be tinkering with some maintenance issue somewhere within earshot – in your clothing, posture and facial expression, but what she will really want to know about you is your name. Mrs Grot's past triumphs at predicting guests' personalities from their names inspire many a dinner-party anecdote.

You can imagine her glee one blustery April afternoon when she realised that Hillary Starcross, Victoria Winner and Sybil Wimpey were due to arrive. It was easy for her to inform her husband of what he must expect.

'Hillary Starcross – a theatrical type. He'll be demanding and over-sensitive, as in my opinion actors always are. I won't have much time for him. Victoria Winner – now, *there's* a strong name. I predict we're going to like her. She'll be a big personality and game for some fun. Sybil Wimpey – well, the surname says it all, doesn't it? Don't need to pay much attention to her.'

'They're all staying for one night only,' ventured Mr Grot, with a raise of the eyebrows that indicated this fact was significant.

'Yes, I know, and we're reaching the end of the week when our Important Guest promised to come for a night. But if it's any of these three, it can only be Victoria. If we focus our attention on her, we'll have no cause for concern.'

Mr Grot would have liked to remind her one could never be too careful with any guest in this age of online reviews, but he knew better than to dare.

The first arrival, wheeling a neat black travel case, was Victoria Winner. When the Grots opened the door, she beamed at them and presented a confident hand to be shaken. She wore a trouser-suit and her hair was chopped into a practical, short style. Mrs Grot greatly approved of this lack of frivolity.

'I'm here for an interview,' explained Victoria to Mrs Grot's fawning enquiries over the special privilege of a complimentary welcoming coffee. 'My ambition is to bring the Victoria Winner brand into open dialogue with other stakeholders in the empowerment industry. I believe that many individuals aren't making enough use of their personal power to succeed in today's society. I have a desire to actualise my ability to help these individuals, so I'm applying for a coaching course.'

Mrs Grot was unfamiliar with some of Victoria's phraseology, but it was all said stridently enough that she retained high hopes of building a rapport. 'Oh, yes, there are a lot of useless types around nowadays, aren't there? They need to buck up.'

Victoria's eyes widened with an emotion that, had she not been so strapping, might have resembled alarm, but she quickly recovered herself.

'I can see this is an environment where honest expression of one's thoughts is a key value. I validate that value and I'll make best use of my personal power to uphold it during my stay.'

Upon finishing her coffee, she was invited upstairs to her room, but declined, explaining that a preliminary viewing of the interview's location was a stepping-stone to interview success. Mr Grot whisked away her travel case and promised it would be waiting by her bed when she returned. Neither he nor his wife expected she would be absent for long. 'If she's got the determination to apply for this course of hers, you can bet she's got the drive to keep up a side career,' he surmised with one foot on the staircase. 'She'll need to spend time sampling our services. She's Important all right.'

'What did I say before?' smirked Mrs Grot. 'Analysing people is really very easy.'

The second arrival of the day was a portly, balding pensioner, who huffed and spluttered his way into the hallway with a brown leather holdall.

'Good afternoon, good afternoon! How do you do? Awful traffic out there! Finally here, though! Very much looking forward to a break!'

'I'm ever so sorry, but we have no vacancies left for tonight,' replied Mrs Grot.

'Oh? But I reserved a room! Hillary Starcross. I booked! There must be some mistake.'

'Hillary Starcross?' Both the Grots said it, he with politeness, she with frustrated disbelief.

'May I ask why you're staying here?' she added while Mr Grot tapped on the computer keyboard. 'A trip to the theatre, perhaps?'

'The theatre?' Mr Starcross giggled. 'Oh no, not me. I've only come for a change of scene. Just a bit of relaxation. A quiet night, hopefully. I'm an easy-going sort.'

Mrs Grot uttered not another word until the check-in was complete and the elderly guest had tottered off to his room. Then she marched into the kitchen and slammed the door.

Mr Grot hoped fervently that Sybil Wimpey would be wimpy enough to placate her.

Time rolled on. Victoria returned from her expedition full of resolution and hurried upstairs to rehearse standard competency questions, refusing offers of another complimentary drink because her metabolism was currently not requiring hydration. Hillary sipped and sighed his way through several cups of tea in the Relaxation Lounge, while exploring the variety of magazines and television channels on offer. The Grots began to wonder if Sybil would ever come.

'Time for dinner,' announced Mrs Grot. 'If she misses it, it's her own fault.'

The two guests had just sat down to the Sunshine Bistro's speciality of Battered Cod and Salted Potato Segments, Acquired From a Local Source, when the doorbell rang. Mrs Grot stomped off to answer it and came back grinning radiantly.

Dragging an enormous lilac box across the carpet was a waif-like figure with an expression of woe. Suddenly, she stopped and let out a wail.

'I don't know what to do! Oh, *where* can I put my case? I worry so much if it isn't stored with five metres of air on all sides. If it's stored any other way, it might feel squashed!'

Ordinarily, awkward requests from guests made Mrs Grot snappy, but that evening her delight shone through as she exclaimed, 'Well, I'm not at all sure there'll be space for that! Dear me!'

Mr Grot sidled out of the kitchen and his reaction to Sybil was less triumphant. He blushed, nodded, scratched his head and scurried back in again.

Sybil stared at him for a moment, then dropped into the nearest chair and murmured, 'I desperately need some dinner.'

'No problem,' chuckled Mrs Grot. 'Our speciality at the Sunshine Bistro is Battered Cod with…'

'Cod? Oh, no. I'm a fruitarian. As in, I only eat fruit that has fallen naturally from a tree.'

'*What?*'

'You do cater for dietary requirements, don't you?'

'I can't say we're used to them, Miss Wimpey. We offer a British delicacy here which most guests find delightful.'

'Try a Salted Potato Segment,' offered Hillary, waving one of his in Sybil's direction. 'It's very superior. Looks like a chip, but something about it's just better. Can't put my finger on it.'

'The Segments have a strong and positive effect on my sense of taste,' added Victoria. 'And see how large my portion is. Mrs Grot is really fostering my appetite.'

Mr Grot's red face had appeared at the kitchen door again. 'Perhaps Sybil might like some of those blackcurrants we got from that shrub in the yard last autumn?'

Mrs Grot led her husband into the kitchen for a discreet word. 'Firstly, we picked them, they didn't fall off, and secondly, why should we bother to pander to her fussy ways? She's almost wimpier than I imagined, which is saying something. Make her do as she's told.'

'I totally see your point, but…'

'Come on, she's obviously not Important! We have nothing to worry about in that quarter! And even if she posts on what-do-you-call-it, one of those websites, people will take one look at her wimpy photo and they won't bother a jot about what she says. People respect a strong personality.'

'You have a strong personality, my love.' Mr Grot knew his script.

'I do. And I can read people and I know what they need. One day she'll thank me for making her buck up and eat the fish and chips. Don't forget to make a note of what you paid at the chip shop tonight, by the way. No, in the meantime, we've got her money and that's the bottom line for a businesswoman like me.'

She marched out again, refusing to register the nervousness spreading across her husband's face.

After Sybil had sobbed her way through her Cod and Segments and picked at an Eton Tidy ('Like Eton Mess, but without the strawberries or cream – just the meringue, my favourite bit!' to use Hillary's definition), she was not invited to an Entertainment Night in the Relaxation Lounge with her fellow guests.

'We're going to watch a grown-up series that she won't cope with,' muttered Mrs Grot to Victoria in a conspiratorial manner. 'So don't let on that you and Hillary have been invited.'

Victoria frowned. 'Could you qualify that word 'grown-up' for me? Say, in terms of cognitive development stages? My meaning is, what specifically is it that you believe is incompatible with her temperament?'

'Oh, the shocking language, the themes, you know. It's very much our sense of humour, but it won't be hers. You'll like it, with your big personality.'

'I see.' If the lighting in the hallway had not been so dim, one could have said that Victoria looked rather pale.

The chosen two gathered in the Relaxation Lounge at the appointed time and found they had been allocated an area on the carpet in which to sit.

'Mr Grot and I need the sofas,' explained Mrs Grot. 'This the highlight of our week – our only respite, in fact, from all the cooking and cleaning that is the hotelier's lot.'

'I'm sure you work very hard,' replied Hillary in a comforting tone.

'Recreational moments are key in the lives of all people,' commented Victoria.

Mr Grot switched on the television in the midst of the opening credits. Names were trundling across the screen in a copperplate font, accompanied by lush string music and a serene rural backdrop.

'You wait!' he guffawed. 'This is just setting the scene!'

The title of the programme appeared to be *Bridge to Happiness.*

Several elderly characters shuffled out of their thatched village homes and met on a cobbled street.

'Today's bridge game should be an exciting one, shouldn't it, Phyllis?' remarked one.

'Without a doubt, Gladys. I'm looking forward to getting my own back on Stanley!'

'Oh, yes! I don't like to speak ill of anyone, but he didn't really deserve to win last week.'

'With whom do you think he'll partner up?'

'Perhaps with Fred? Fred's mathematical ability is second to none. Watch out for them if they do collaborate!'

Mrs Grot emitted a curious snort and leant over to nudge Victoria. 'Fabulous, isn't it? You understand what they're getting at?'

'Yes, of course. The theme is clearly adult.'

'That's my girl! Mr Grot and I knew you were our type!'

The cameras cut to the group of friends entering a church hall and pondering over which of a cluster of square tables to sit at. A man with a bulging stomach who was already ensconced at one of them heaved himself up and waved.

'Oh Gladys, you have to admit, Stanley is rather friendly. He waved at me last week too, and then after the match he offered to make me a cup of tea.'

'Really, Phyllis!'

'A cup of tea!' shrieked Mr Grot, collapsing with laughter onto his wife's shoulder. 'Dread to think! The mind boggles!'

'It's Fred's mathematical ability that gets me!' guffawed Mrs Grot. 'Anyone with a bit of worldly experience can guess what that means, and it's not an image I'm likely to forget in a hurry!'

While the Grots were producing this level of noise, Hillary took the opportunity to whisper to Victoria, 'I realise I'm not a member of the trendy younger generation, but I've seen this programme before, and unless I'm very much mistaken, it can be taken at face value. I think it's just about a group of friends playing bridge.'

Victoria gazed at Hillary, then at the screen, and her face melted into an expression of pure relief.

'You don't like the sort of content they're desperate to find?' Hillary asked.

'Well, I...'

Victoria was unable to progress any further with her sentence, because at that moment the door burst open. In the empty frame was a desolate Sybil, holding the door handle, which she seemed to have broken off in her anxiety to enter the room.

'You're enjoying yourselves without *me!*' she whined. 'Why wasn't I informed?'

Mrs Grot rose and attempted to bustle her into the hallway. 'This is beyond your comfort zone and I don't think you're ready to be exposed to it.'

With an unexpectedly strong lunge, Sybil bypassed Mrs Grot. Putting out her hand for balance as she defiantly sat down on the carpet, she brushed the top of Victoria's head. Victoria's practical short hair slid to the ground in a single droop, revealing a profusion of long blonde ringlets underneath.

'A wig! By golly, you wouldn't have guessed that, would you?' grinned Mr Grot at Hillary. He then cleared his throat and strove to look very serious while Mrs Grot fixed Victoria with a momentous stare.

'I can appreciate the need for discretion,' she intoned, 'but I think it's reached the point where an open acknowledgement of what you're *really* doing here would be simpler for all concerned. No need for an anonymous letter on our desk when you leave. Come on. Tell us now.'

'I, well, I said I'm here for an interview,' gabbled a shaky Victoria, 'and I am, but there are expectations in today's society and it's impossible, I mean it's challenging, to meet them when you love pink things and afternoon tea and all you really want to do in your spare time is embroider and watch period dramas.'

'I don't understand what that has to do with...'

'Coaches are supposed to be feisty! They're supposed to reject pink as a non-gender-neutral colour and live up to a name like Victoria Winner. I was only trying to develop a modern and role-appropriate personality. Please don't take offence.'

'I think I like you better when you're honest,' interrupted Sybil, 'and I'm pretty sure there are people of all kinds around who share your interests. You don't have to squash yourself because a certain type of character' – she shot a narrow glance at Mrs Grot – 'seems intent on categorising everyone with minimal effort.'

'None of this introspection is of any interest to me,' fumed Mrs Grot. 'You've paid for your room and it has become clear that our relationship ends there. Hillary, can I tempt you with a complimentary cocktail?'

Realising that the free drinks, large portions and cosy chats she had lavished on Victoria had all been the result of a delusion, Mrs Grot was anxious to give proper attention to who she believed was the only possible remaining candidate for Importance. Thanks to his comments about the Sunshine Bistro menu, she suspected Hillary was already enjoying his stay, but in order to be certain, she made him brunch in bed the next morning and provided him with her own and Mr Grot's company throughout. They announced themselves by singing the Broadway show-tune *Good Morning* through his bedroom door, and Mrs Grot had a wonderful laugh at Mr

Grot's attempts to relate the lyrics to the sort of hard-hitting storylines found in *Bridge to Happiness.*

'Well, many thanks for a fascinating stay,' huffed Hillary as he staggered downstairs later on to settle his bill. 'It's certainly been one of my more memorable holidays.'

'I'm so glad. We're always delighted to have our services evaluated by a real connoisseur.'

'I've found it very memorable too,' murmured Sybil, who was hovering in the hallway with her case. 'And thankfully my case has just about survived.'

'A change in storage conditions won't hurt it at all. I expect you want us to call you a taxi so you don't have to carry it to the station?'

'No, thank you. I'll be taking the bus back to Headington. My home isn't far away, you see.'

'How very adventurous. I suppose leaving town for your holiday would overwhelm you?'

A non-bewigged Victoria scurried downstairs, her head drooping with embarrassment. She silently paid her bill, nodded at Hillary and the Grots, and told Sybil with a wan smile, 'I've thought about what you said last night. Thank you. It's a different kind of empowerment, and I might even explore it at my interview.'

Suddenly, all three guests were gone. As they said their goodbyes, Mrs Grot stared at Victoria's ringlets and inwardly marvelled at how anyone called Victoria Winner could possibly look like that. This was probably why she failed to notice someone slip a letter onto the reception desk.

It was from the Hotel Evaluation Association. It informed her, as she had anticipated, that an Evaluator had stayed at her property the previous night and would be publishing their official review and rating shortly.

'As Important Guests go, I quite liked Hillary,' she remarked to Mr Grot. 'I predict we've no worries there. We managed to give him a theatrical element with our show-tune. Now, he may have said he wasn't visiting the theatre this time, but I've no doubt that he goes when he's at home. Strictly as a spectator, obviously. He's too easy-going to be an actor. I think we can safely assume I was half-right.'

Mr Grot sighed.

'And Victoria, well, the less said, the better. At least she was aware of what she *ought* to be. And Sybil I can't be bothered to discuss. Wimpy and forgettable, she was. One of my easier guesses.'

At the bus stop outside St Clement's Church, an anxious-looking woman in a pink silk suit stepped off the No 13 and Sybil Wimpey stepped on. She settled herself in a side seat and plonked her case carelessly in the tight space allocated for luggage, wheelchairs and pushchairs. From her coat pocket she pulled a notebook and a pen. As the bus rumbled along, she scribbled some ideas for the next report she would write in her capacity as Oxford Area Officer for the Hotel Evaluation Association. What a lot she had to say. She had known something was, as it were, fishy when she recognised her host as the man sneaking out the local fish and chip shop laden with dinners while she dragged her case down the road; his wife's consistent rudeness, unfounded assumptions and raucous brunch-time vocals had only worsened her impression.

Her colleagues called her the toughest reviewer in the land, with her repertoire of bizarre requirements that she used to test candidates' customer service skills. She really wasn't at all wimpy, but unfortunately for Mr and Mrs Grot, she had decided after her night's experience that their establishment was rather grotty.

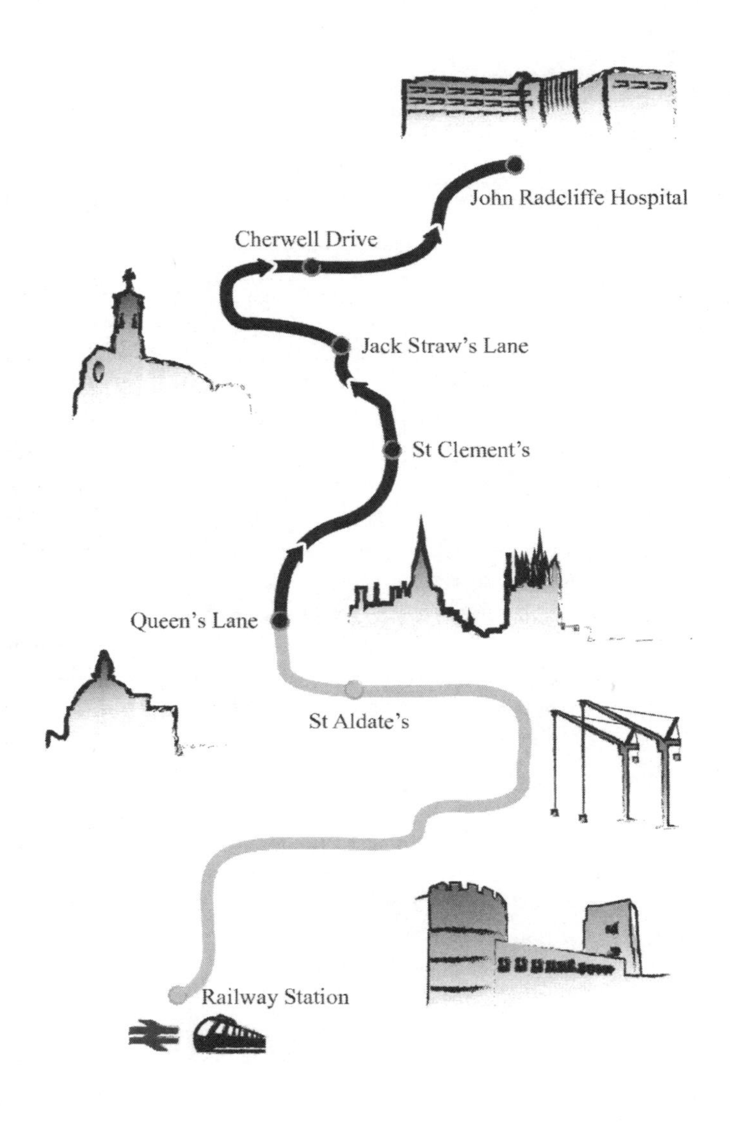
John Radcliffe Hospital
Cherwell Drive
Jack Straw's Lane
St Clement's
Queen's Lane
St Aldate's
Railway Station

A Short History of Oxford

REBECCA HOTCHEN

Tap. Tap. Tap. Thump. Peter's stick finds solid purchase. He uses it to haul himself up, like a mountaineer pulling against a rope to reach a summit. 'Right you are, Peter,' the driver says in greeting. 'Up to see your missus, is it?'

'It is indeed,' Peter says. 'And how do you think of these for her?' He brandishes the bouquet he's just bought. Some petals have been blown off in the walk down the High Street from the covered market, but Sally has smiled at more battered and bruised gifts than these. 'Purple's her favourite colour, you know.'

'A stunning arrangement,' the driver says.

Peter shuffles forward. Stick. Left foot. Right foot. Stick. Left foot. Right foot. He doesn't sit in the very first chair he comes to; he needs to be looking forward. Not that he'll miss his stop, no worry of that. He's been on the No 13 bus a thousand times before and he knows the route by heart. No, he just likes to see what's coming. He doesn't want to watch the city vanish behind them.

Peter is one of the first ones on. He often is these days; it's age before beauty, he knows. He doesn't mind sitting and letting himself get comfortable while the other passengers file on. When was it? Not too long ago, he's sure, and Sally is sitting beside him. They take the bus together to most of her appointments. She says she can get herself up there and down again without a chaperone, she's a grown woman by now at least, but Peter insists it's for his sake. 'And what sort of trouble would I get into without you keeping an eye on me?' he asks and she laughs. Her laugh never changes. Of course, her voice breaks and weakens and cracks, and the lines around her mouth have grown from mere suggestions to undeniable facts, but the motion is always the same, her hand half lifting as though to cover her mouth, and her voice a song. Peter loves making her laugh. She leans against him while her breath comes back to her, and his arm comes round her like they are a couple of kids sitting in the darkened hall of a cinema. He steals a quick kiss.

The bus begins to move and the seat next to Peter is empty. It looks wrong, so Peter lays his bouquet there, the purple clashing against bold red patterned fabric. He'll not forget it getting off because no one could miss it. The bus glides away, sailing peacefully for only moments before hitting the first lights. Sally has all the patience in the world for lights. She says, once, that it's like being the photograph, with the rest of the world moving around you. Peter teases her for trying to be deep. They aren't married yet and she is more easily embarrassed. Her cheeks colour prettily, and she laughs uncertainly. Peter lifts the uncertainty away with a squeeze of her small hand in his. 'The only deep thoughts I have are about you,' he says, half serious and half joking. He's giving her the chance for retaliation. Maybe she tries to be deep, but his attempts to be romantic… Well! Extraordinarily corny. But she isn't taking the bait. She smiles, instead, and the serious half grows and eclipses the joking half. He means it with all sincerity, like a vow.

The colour shifts to green. A few cyclists nip in front of the bus, keeping them at a snail's pace as they pull over Magdalen Bridge. In the water that passes below, Peter and Sally pedal a boat made for two, undulating back and forth as they struggle to match pace with each other. It is a warm day, and Peter's jacket lies folded under his seat. Sally wears a straw hat woven through with purple flowers. They are out of breath from pedalling. 'Let's just get ourselves out of the way,' Sally says, 'then we can stop for a drink.' They try to take themselves gently to the side, but with a *crash* Peter sees he misjudged the distance. Giving up on the pedals, he pushes against the wall to line the boat up. Other idle boaters sweep past, but they are nothing more than the ducks or the reeds to Peter. He is waiting for Sally to reach into the picnic basket.

'Oh!' she exclaims. She draws out a bottle of champagne. 'Peter, why…?'

'Ten years ago, along this same river, you said you'd marry me. I think that's worth a little bubbly.' The fizz goes to their heads, and as much trouble as they had getting the boat out, it is ten times worse trying to get back. They are both giggling, fifteen minutes past the rental time, as they pull up to the dock. They have better luck with the punting, and next summer they are back to that old way of getting along. They don't explore too far down the river; there is nothing down there they have not seen before. But for the odd push to guide, Peter is happy to let the water set her own pace, and for them to go with her, so that his gaze can stay with Sally and her transfixing smile. A great gust of wind catches her hat and carries it—

Peter flies out of his seat to the sound of a horn. He is unsteady lifting himself up. He thinks his knees might be grazed, as though he is a boy again and prone to climbing trees and dropping out of them. Another passenger comes to help him up, and to gather up his flowers. A few have slid loose of the arrangement. He isn't sure where they go, and he so wanted them to be perfect for Sally. There are more petals gone. His eyes burn. Her flowers should be the best.

She's kneeling in the garden, surrounded by pools of mud. It streaks her hair and her face like warpaint. Rain crashes to the earth in sheets. 'They're all going to be ruined,' she wails. 'They're too young.' Peter kneels beside her helplessly. He watches her desperately transfer the plants back from earth to terracotta, but he knows that his clumsy hands would make them worse than the storm had. 'I should have waited a few more weeks to plant them.'

'We can buy more,' Peter soothes, his lips against her ear so the words are not carried into the distance by the wind. She turns to him, shivering. He puts his dinner jacket over her bare arms and folds her into a hug. The fine silk of her dress will never be the same again. She looks as beautiful in it now, sodden and drowned and coated in mud, as she did magnificently made up, hair elegantly coiled, basking in the soft lights of the ballroom.

'But Peter, if I can't even look after the flowers, how can I ever be a mother?'

She's a natural. Baby William lies in her arms as though he has been nowhere else, as though they were carved as one from the same oak. Both lie with eyes closed against a beam of sun breaking in through the blinds to bathe them in a golden glow. Peter is quiet, a visitor to a fine art gallery, admiring the depth of colour and the long flowing lines.

A young woman boards the bus without paying, struggling up the aisle, her movements awkward with the weight of pregnancy, and her bag bumps against the seats as she passes them. A man boards after her, his money escaping his grasp and rolling away. Peter jumps slightly as a boot comes down hard on the coin to stop its journey. He supposes that this man must be the baby's father from the anxious way his eyes dart to follow the pregnant woman's progress up the aisle.

Peter and Sally grasp each other's hands at the dining table, tears welling in their eyes. A mirror to them, Will and his wife Victoria sit on the other side, not saying a word, but conveying it all with their bodies, bent towards each other like flowers leaning towards light. Their faces have worn soft smiles all through dinner. Finally, Victoria speaks. 'You've guessed by now, I'm sure, but I might as well say it: I'm pregnant!'

William and Victoria have been married for eight years, and Peter knows that they have been trying for a baby for some time. Victoria stands, and there it is, a slight swell to her stomach, and inside a new life that is already so desperately loved. Sally is rushing around the dinner table, and wraps Victoria in her arms. Peter follows, and he claps Will on the back before drawing him in. 'Congratulations,' he whispers.

There are joggers on the open field to Peter's right. He sees them as tiny figures of men, far in the distance. They do not see him at all, he is an organ of the bus no more to be distinguished than his heart or liver can be distinguished from him. Though the day is blustery, they still wear shorts. Lany is covered head to foot in layers of wool. Will carries her on his shoulders as they weave through the crowd. Her legs are already tired, and they have only been out half an hour. 'We always arrive too early,' Peter says, his eyes on the great volcano of wood. It will not erupt for many hours yet, and his granddaughter may be sleeping by then, nestled in Will's coat against the chill of the November elements. Lany has spotted a ride she wants to go on. Sally fumbles for her camera, waving to Lany and her mother Victoria as they come round. Lany is grinning, her face smeared with sauce. It is a wonder she is not sick. Peter remarks as much to Sally, who pulls a face, but does not move away, letting Peter lean on her instead of the walking stick, which slides in the trodden down mud. Lany's face is brighter than the sky, her eyes shining with awe, as she takes in the colours that ignite the gloaming. Sally and Peter do not look at the sky; it is Will, and Victoria, and tiny Lany, who fill them with wonder.

The bus is sailing up Marston Road. He catches a glimpse of a primary school to his right, its colourful fence drawing a margin around a yard in which some older children play a game of rounders. Will triumphs at the egg and spoon race. He has all of his mother's grace and none of Peter's clumsiness. The sun is beating down, and between every competition, parents call children over and reapply the sunscreen. Will wriggles in protest, glancing at the other boys in his class to make sure they don't see him, but allows it. He zips away to take part in the next race, a relay, taking his position two thirds of the way along the track and looking serious and intent as the whistle is blown.

The bell rings. The bus pulls into a stop. Peter does not see who gets off. He is gazing at the small church just behind them, his neck turned. Lany is in white and lace and is angry about the whole thing. Her tiny face is red and wet. Her protests echo through the church hall, and the older guests all smile. Her cries are cut off by a sprinkle of water touching her head. Startled, her dark eyes spring open. This is the moment in the silver frame resting on Sally's sewing table, and Sally puts her project down often to gaze at it. 'She's walking already,' Sally comments. 'Can you believe it?' Peter slides a finger into his book to mark his place and turns to his wife.

'I can hardly believe it of Will. Seems only yesterday *he* was being dunked in a font. How does he have one of his own already?'

The bus stops often now, as they reach the houses. People who are not Sally are going home for the evening. The bus will be pulling into the hospital soon, and Peter puts his hand on his bouquet to make sure he doesn't forget it. The stems are cold and wet beneath his fingers, anchoring him to the present.

Peter allows the others to get off the bus first. The driver lowers the platform for someone with a pram. With the bus kneeling, Peter can start his shuffle-stop-shuffle towards the exit.

'You give your wife my best, now,' the driver says, and Peter promises he will. It is not far to the main entrance, which is lucky, as the flowers cannot take any more of the elements.

The smell that greets Peter is a familiar one. He lifts his bruised flowers to his nose and inhales their perfume instead. That's better. The receptionist greets him, but not with her usual smile. Her mouth is pulled down, as though the weight of the world rests in the lines of her face. She touches a hand to his elbow gently.

Peter closes his eyes. It is bad that she is gentle.

'I'm here to see Sally,' he says, just like the last time he was here and the time before, but it is wrong. A few months ago, she is admitted to the hospital during an appointment. Her test results concern the doctor, who is looking at the page and scowling as though it has insulted her personally.

Sally is smiling and saying she's sure there's nothing to worry about, but Peter knows that she is worried, and Peter is worried too. There is a wobble to her smile that he's seen before in waiting rooms. 'I'll come every day,' Peter says to Sally, 'until you're well enough to come home again.' He wraps an old arm around her old shoulders.

Until she's well enough to come home again. It is months and he visits her every day at this time, and he brings her flowers if hers have faded, and they sit, and he watches her fade too.

'Peter,' a kind, gentle voice says now with him in the reception area. Oh, it is too cruel that it is so kind and gentle. It always means the worst. Yesterday the room is all sharp, curt voices and sharp, curt movements, and he is hustled out with no gentleness while Sally's machines all sing out to the heavens. Peter watches these violent bursts of activity explode around his wife and sees the purpose in them like a clairvoyant reading signs in tea leaves. It is a comfort. Then the voices quieten. The movements slow. The purpose is lost from both. Sally's machines wail rather than sing. Peter cannot see; there are too many bodies in the way. A hand touches his shoulder gently, and Peter learns the danger in being gentle, when soft soft words explain to him that Sally is gone.

Only one day passes and everything is different; the world is a changed place. Will is coming up from London today to be with his father, and Victoria and Lany will follow at the weekend, solemn and quiet. Yesterday Peter sees Sally smile one last time. Today he forgets that the world is a whole new place with no more of her smiles in it.

'I brought these for the nurses,' he lies. 'As a thank you. I know… I know you all did right by her while she...'

He doesn't finish. He doesn't wait. He doesn't want to be in this place any longer. Sally is not here, pale against pale sheets. She is not reading quietly in the library while Peter indecisively looks over the shelves in case he's missed a better book, not visiting with Will and sipping tea, not boating along the river under Magdalen Bridge, not pushing her granddaughter on a swing. She is not in the home she has shared with Peter for fifty years. She is not coming home.

Peter twists the wedding band on his finger as he waits. The wind pummels him and he is glad for it. It lets him draw his hat down low to coax shadows over his eyes. If the bus comes soon, he might make it to the train station in time to meet Will. He longs for his son's sturdy presence. The space next to him is still warm and full. It's not had time to cool. The echo of her hand still grips his, and he still sees her wobbly smile become strong when he produces a bunch of purple flowers with most of their petals intact. He has not had time to change his ways. He'll learn. The pillar-box red 13 pulls up and Peter boards alone.

oxford

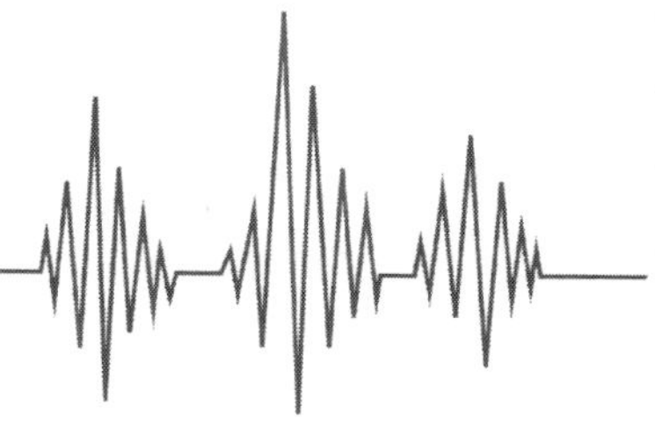

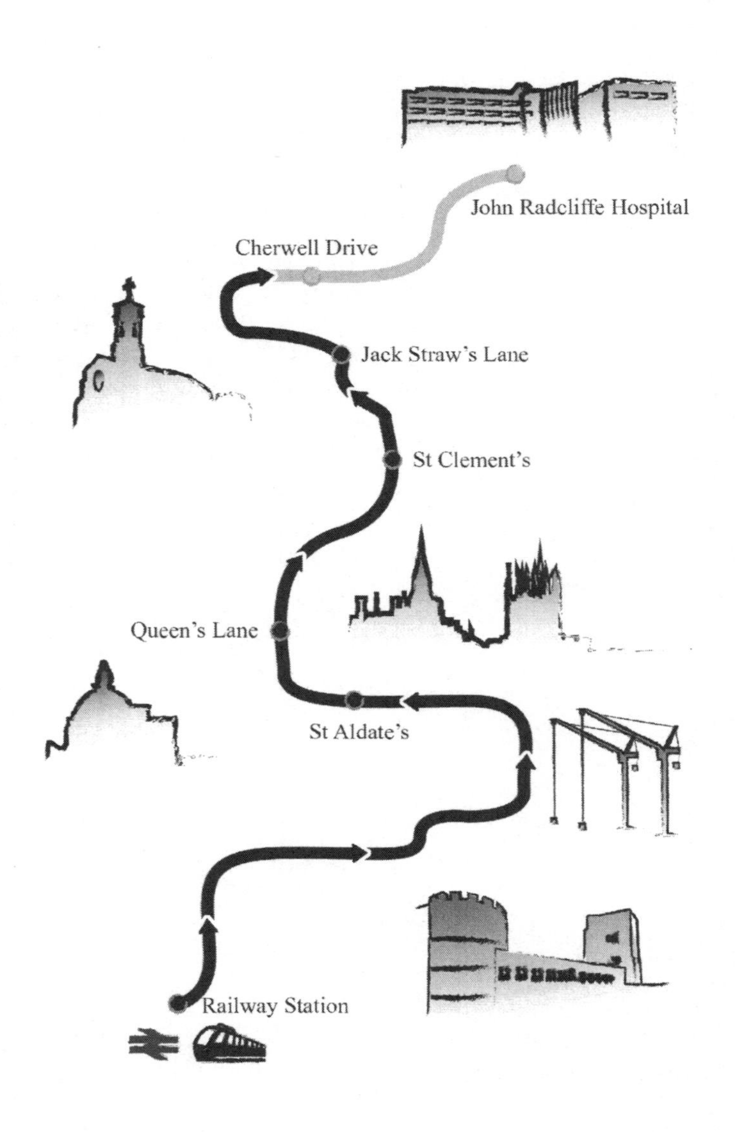
John Radcliffe Hospital
Cherwell Drive
Jack Straw's Lane
St Clement's
Queen's Lane
St Aldate's
Railway Station

Trilby

OLIVER NESHAM

As the train slowed down for Oxford, Colin's sinking feeling hit rock bottom. In recent years his visits to his daughter had become more a duty than a pleasure, and rarer as a consequence. Julia no longer made the trip to the family home because, she said, Streatham was boring. But she still expected her aging father to take the train, the tube and train again to spend an uncomfortable few days cooped up in her dilapidated terraced house off Cowley Road. He suspected he was the only one who had a bedroom to himself because the house was always full. There were Julia's two boys – completely out of control of course and, usually, one or two unexplained characters who left as mysteriously as they came. He was never introduced to them.

Colin had been a widower for long enough to become used to his own company. He was perfectly capable of looking after himself but, for some reason, Julia had taken it upon herself to mother him. Julia - of all people. As an only child she had been the focus of all the love, attention and opportunity that her parents could provide. But as she grew into a teenager Colin felt that his wife tried too hard to be a modern mother. There were whispered conversations in which, he assumed, he was the subject; they derided his conservative values, the way he dressed and his dedication to his clients. When they were in full flow Julia adopted a particularly irritating tone of voice, which his wife began to imitate.

At university Julia got mixed up with the wrong crowd, dropped out in her second year and went travelling in South

America. Three years later she came back with a greasy gaucho in tow; Colin suspected he was a drug-dealer and that he was the father of Julia's oldest son. Not that it mattered; the gaucho was a distant memory now and there followed a succession of other men, including the father of her second son. Fortunately all that happened in Oxford where, Colin supposed, everyone behaved like that.

Retrieving his hat, mackintosh, furled umbrella and case from the luggage rack, Colin stepped onto the platform. He fumbled with the mobile phone Julia had given him for Christmas. He had never used it and couldn't see the point of it; indeed, he now realised, he hadn't charged it up. In vain he looked around for a public telephone. But does it matter, he asked himself. He was only pandering to Julia's demand that he should ring when he reached Oxford 'to stop her worrying'. She wasn't going to be at home in any case; he had instructions to let himself in with the key under the doormat. Julia would be involved in 'case reviews' all day - whatever they were. When asked she variously described herself as a social worker, a researcher or an editor although, as far as Colin was aware, her modest income was mainly derived from working in a vegan restaurant.

The No 13 was purring at its stand and Colin asked the driver to tell him when they reached Marston - Ferry Road, Julia's new address. 'You will love it', she promised over the telephone, 'it's got a granny flat, and you can have it all to yourself – stay as long as you like!' Colin was appalled on two counts: first that he was expected to suffer the indignity of occupying a 'granny' flat, and, second, that he was expected to stay rather longer this time. 'You can instill some discipline into those brats of mine,' Julia laughed gaily. There had been more than a hint recently that a permanent move to Oxford might be a good idea so that 'we can keep an eye on you'. Colin shuddered at the thought.

He sat downstairs on the back seat. In front of him sat the kind of specimen he saw all too often in Streatham. A male of the species, wearing a baseball cap back-to-front, tattoos up his arms and with his feet up on the seat opposite. And, of course, he was fiddling with an electronic device of some kind. Colin sighed and thought of Streatham. He had lived there all his life; even when he got married he only moved around the corner. But it was different now; most of his neighbours were foreign and the house was too big for him; it also needed a good deal spending on it. Still, it was his. He had managed to pay off the mortgage early through his diligent work as an insurance salesman, enabling him to give Julia a good start in life. Now she found that all rather amusing and teased him about the way he achieved his success.

For Colin had a way with the ladies. No smutty intimacies – not that kind of thing at all. Just old-fashioned courtesies and an easy eloquence; he was the perfect gentleman. He always wore a dark suit, white shirt, sober tie and black shoes, polished daily. He also wore a trilby which he raised in greeting to every woman he recognised. It delighted them and he soon built up an enviable portfolio of female clients, widows mostly, anxious to secure their future. His respectable bearing, quiet confidence and, it must be said, the twinkle in his eye, earned him a reputation which was spread by word of mouth. Colin believed the trilby was the key to his success and still wore one as a kind of talisman.

No other trilbies on the bus today, he noted. In fact, apart from Mr Baseball and a woman dressed entirely in pink whose hat had been blown off as she boarded the bus, there were no hats at all. Although he could see them only from the back his fellow passengers seemed to be a pretty ordinary lot. Then he noticed a sweet little girl sitting nearby. She seemed to be on her own and, in more civilised times, he would have talked to her. But these days... The bus went through a large construction site overshadowed by some massive, white cranes, and he wondered what was going on there. But then they were in the university area; he admired the architecture and its history of course, but it always seemed a bit unreal to him, and it attracted the strangest mix of people. No wonder Julia found a home here.

The bus turned down a leafy road which soon passed through endless, uniform housing, and Colin began to feel more at home. It was in just such locations that he had built up his loyal base of clients. After a while the bus driver turned and called, 'Marston Ferry Road next stop,' and he gathered up his possessions. 'On the left at the junction; we turn right for the hospital.' Colin thanked him, alighted and made for the road indicated.

It was not at all what he expected. It was almost open countryside. There was a lot of fast-moving traffic but the pavement and a cycle track ran behind a high mound and a hedge. If he wasn't carrying his case it would be quite a pleasant walk. But the strange thing was – there was no sign of houses. Colin continued walking.

Presently he found himself approaching a line of trees where the road crossed a river. Under a large, green umbrella a man sat fishing. A futile occupation, Colin always thought, but it might be something to think about if the worst came to the worst and he ended up living with Julia. Later on he noticed some allotments on the other side of the road. Something else for him to do: he had always fancied growing vegetables but had been discouraged by the overgrown shrubs and scrubby lawn that constituted his garden back in Streatham. His case was beginning to feel rather heavy now. If he knew that Julia lived this far out he would have taken a taxi.

Then civilisation came into view; first there were sports fields, then schools on either side of the road and, eventually, blocks of flats. One of them was called Marston Ferry Court, a reassuring sign to Colin who was beginning to wonder if he was still on the right road. Beyond them there were houses and a busy road junction.

He stopped outside No 15. It was in a terrace of substantial, recently-built town houses. This was definitely a step up for Julia and he wondered if he had misjudged her.

He opened the gate and lifted the door mat. No key. Typical. Thinking she may have got home earlier than expected, he rang the bell.

The person who answered the door was an elegant, middle-aged lady. Instinctively, Colin raised his trilby with a little bow and asked if Julia was at home. There must be some mistake; there was no Julia here – and yes, this was Marston Ferry Road. His upright poise slumped; suddenly his case felt very heavy and he felt utterly dejected. 'You look done in. Why don't you come in – I was just putting the kettle on and we can sort out the problem.' She sat him in a comfortable, book-lined study.

After introductions – her name was Sheila – they sipped their tea and considered the situation. Colin learned that he was actually in Summertown; that there were all the shops you need just around the corner – bars and restaurants too, a doctor's surgery and a gym just across the road and buses into Oxford every few minutes; indeed the No 14 stopped just outside and ran all the way to the station. Sheila moved in only a year ago and loved it. But there was no Julia.

'I think,' she said, 'you have fallen for one of Oxford's little tricks.'

Tricks? What kind of place is this? Colin wondered, all his prejudices about the city returning.

'For example, we have a South Parade just north of here and a North Parade to the south. There is also a Ferry Road, Marston as well as a Marston Ferry Road – and the No 13 bus passes both.'

Colin groaned. 'And is this Ferry Road close to shops, bars, restaurants, a doctor's surgery and gym?'

Sheila paused before answering, then said, 'No.'

Julia will love this, he thought. Perfect evidence that he needed her to 'keep an eye' on him. He should ring her, he supposed. But he hadn't charged his mobile. More evidence for Julia. Smiling, and seeing his exasperation, Sheila said, 'Try this,' and passed him a proper telephone. Julia was shrill with anger and anxiety. When she had calmed down she told him to stay exactly where he was and she would pick him up. Evidently she had acquired a car.

Sheila was laughing now; she was greatly amused by his account of how he ended up in her home. 'But there must be a lot of people wandering around Oxford like me, hopelessly lost,' he observed.

'There are. We round them up on Wednesdays and auction them in the Gloucester Green slave market.'

'I'm afraid I wouldn't fetch very much.' Sheila studied him.

'No. But if you were a pretty little Chinese tourist...'

The door-bell rang. When she answered it there were shrieks of, 'Julia!' 'Sheila!' They knew each other from the pilates class they both attended. Julia had a few more grey hairs, Colin noted, but she seemed genuinely pleased to see him. She accepted Sheila's invitation to a conducted tour of the house. They were away a long time and Colin overheard their conversation as they went from room to room. Julia was clearly impressed; she had always wanted to live in Summertown, apparently. The identical house next door was coming on the market soon. Colin pricked up his ears; why was Julia talking in that silly tone she used as a teenager? There was hushed conversation about property values in which, he was certain, he heard Streatham mentioned. They discussed rates and schools and when next door might become vacant. 'He can afford it, easily.' That from Julia. 'There's lots for him to do here,' from Sheila. Colin was reminded of the way Julia and her mother used to talk about him as if he wasn't there. Well, he'd had enough of that.

A sudden silence indicated that the tour had now reached the garden. Then, after a few minutes, Julia returned excitedly to the study.

'Dad. We've just had the most fantastic idea...'

But Colin wasn't there. He was on the No 14 bus, heading back to Streatham.

oxford

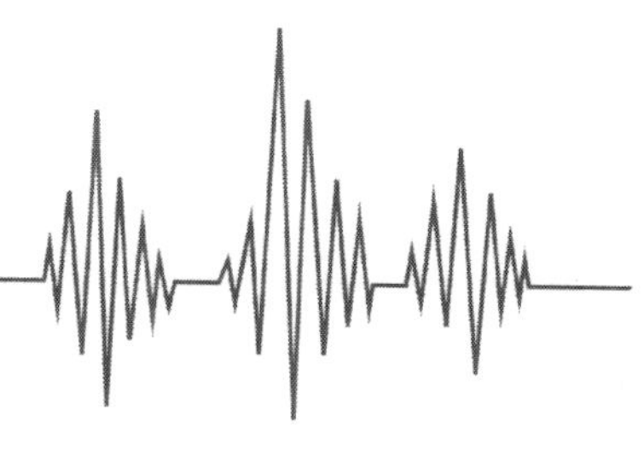

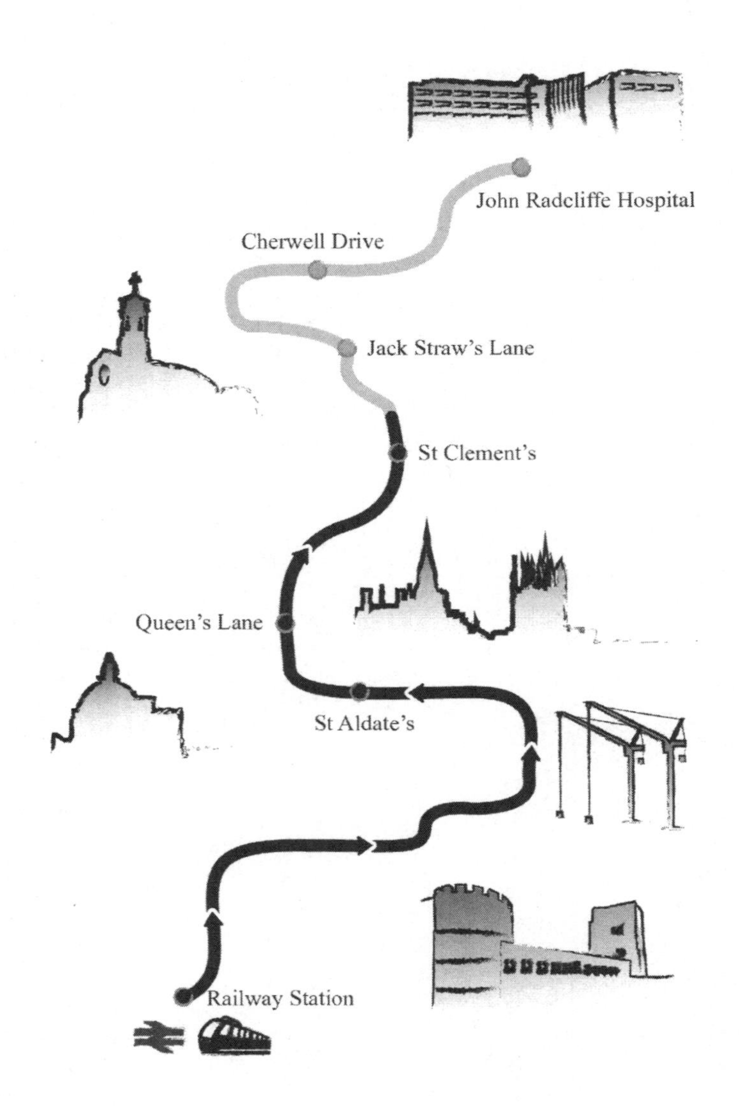
John Radcliffe Hospital
Cherwell Drive
Jack Straw's Lane
St Clement's
Queen's Lane
St Aldate's
Railway Station

The Guest

PAULINE MASSEY

Jill's arrival at the station forecourt was heralded by a blustery wind and she had to hold fast to her tiny hat. In fact the hat was more of a fascinator, with feathers and baubles. In the shop it had looked fetching, now she wasn't convinced of its practicality. Likewise her shoes. She was wobbling on their thin heels and the wind was lashing at her, having fun trying to knock her off her feet. Spring wasn't supposed to be like this, was it? Then Jill reminded herself that it was still early April and there had been a snow flurry last week.

Jill's pink suit looked incongruous among the casually dressed people waiting at the bus stop. Even an older man was wearing jeans and a chunky jumper. Is that what Oxford was like then? Lots of clever people dressed like tramps because they didn't need to go in for 'presentation'? Jill wished her job would allow her to slob around like that.

She glanced at her gold watch. Somehow she was reluctant to take a taxi to the church. Besides, she had loads of time. Jill's train journey from London had been swift and the ceremony wasn't until two thirty. Her best friend getting married after all this time. Jill still couldn't believe it. They hadn't seen one another for ages and then the invitation had arrived out of the blue.

Laura had given her instructions, including details of the No 13 bus from the station. 'Just in case you fancy mixing with the locals rather than being insulated in a taxi,' she had quipped. Same old Laura, Jill thought, still taking the mick.

The older man approached Jill and said, 'Have you got the time? I have a hospital appointment at two fifteen.'

Laura lifted the silk cuff of her pink suit and examined her watch. 'It's twenty past one,' she offered. 'There's a taxi rank over there.'

'I'm all right with the bus usually,' the man said.

At that moment a particularly forceful gust of wind wrenched at Jill's fascinator and sent it skittering across the station forecourt. Jill tried hard to run after it but her shoes were an impediment. Nonetheless she had to catch it. It had cost a fortune and she wanted to look her best.

The crash was unexpected. Down she went, hitting her face against the tarmac. One heel had completely detached itself from her shoe. Jill sat in the middle of the road for a while, stunned. And it was at that moment that the No 13 bus chose to arrive. Jill looked up in time to see her feathered fascinator rising into the air like some bejewelled bird.

The passengers waiting at the bus stop were kind. Two young people and the older man rushed into the road and surrounded her like a protective cordon.

'Anything broken?' The young man was concerned. 'Do you want an ambulance?'

'No, no ambulance, I'm fine, thank you.'

'Let me help you to your feet,' the older man suggested.

Jill could hear the purr of the bus engine until it cut out. She was creating a scene, the last thing she wanted to do. And look at her lovely silk suit. It was stained with dark marks from where she had dropped like a stone onto the road. What a sight she must look. And then she thought of Laura, her best friend from school days, and how she would laugh.

'You look like one of us now, Jill, a bit on the scruffy side.' The remarks weren't meant unkindly. It was just that Laura had always been an arty type and Jill was more strait-laced. Different characters but they'd always got on well.

'Tell you what,' the older man was saying, 'I'm on my way to the hospital. I could show you where to go to get yourself checked over.'

'I'm fine, really.' Jill was on her feet now and holding on to the young man's arm. 'I just need to get to Saint Clement's Church. My best friend is getting married this afternoon.'

The bus driver was kind too. Jill's embarrassment increased as she was made a fuss of and put on one of the seats meant for the disabled. The older man sat next to her.

'Just tell me if you want to carry on to the hospital,' he advised. 'You did go down with a bang.'

As the bus swung round to find its way out of the station area, Jill looked out of the window and saw where her fascinator had landed. She couldn't believe it. It was gracing the back of a large bronze statue of an ox. She considered asking the bus driver to stop while she retrieved it but then decided to leave it where it was. After all, she was dressed in a filthy suit with one heel missing from her shoe and blood oozing from a scratch on her face. What would be the point of trying to look smart now?

A young woman came forward to where Jill was sitting and proffered a packet of tissues.

'Thank you,' Jill said, 'that's really kind.'

She took one out of the packet and pressed it against her cheek where it felt sore. Not only was there dirt on her suit, but the cut on her face had dripped blood on to its collar too.

The elderly man pointed out Oxford's latest shopping development in progress as the No 13 switch-backed its way through building works. He was trying to distract her. Jill peered out of the bus window at looming cranes with men dressed in orange sitting high up in their cabins. She wondered what it would be like being so high up on a day like today with the wind howling. Soon the bus was on its way past huge iron railings and honey-coloured buildings.

'See the blossom there in Christ Church,' her companion said. 'It's struggling in this wind. But what a lovely colour, just like your suit.'

'My suit *was* a lovely colour when I left home this morning,' Jill said with a wry smile.

Once the bus had come to a halt outside a café, Jill pulled out a small mirror from her bag and attempted to tidy her face. Huge eyes looked back at her, shocked. What a sight.

'You'll be all right,' the man said kindly. 'Your friend will just be glad that you made it. She will want you to be with her on her big day.'

In the centre of Oxford there was even more bustle. Tourists were standing at the bottom of a tower, peering upwards, holding their coats against the wind.

'Carfax,' her companion informed her. 'The quarter boys will strike the bells at a quarter to the hour.'

It was already twenty to two. Jill tried not to think of her appearance at the church. At least she was still in reasonable time and could sneak into a back pew before the couple arrived. She would have to take her shoes off, unless she could snap the heel off the other one to even things up. Jill smiled again. She knew what Laura would say about it all, 'The best laid plans, Jill, the best laid plans...'

In the High Street, which Jill remembered from her trip to the city years ago, there were even more tourists. A magnolia was blooming, burgeoning delicate pink cups despite the cruel wind.

'We might have to wait a while at Queen's Lane while the drivers change over,' Jill's companion told her. 'Not long usually.'

'You've been really kind to me,' Jill said to the elderly man. 'Are Oxford people usually this helpful?'

'It depends,' her companion answered and it was his turn to give a wry smile. 'But on the whole, yes. I make this journey every other month. The hospital looks after me well. I'm on the mend now. I'm hoping to help out at the League of Friends café eventually. Your cheek has stopped bleeding, by the way.'

'That's good then,' Jill said. 'I might look like something that the wind's blown in, but hopefully not too much like Dracula's daughter!'

As the No 13 waited for its new driver Jill had another chance to look in her mirror and attempt to tidy up. But she didn't bother. At least Laura would laugh when she heard the story of the errant fascinator and where it had landed up. Jill could just imagine her saying, 'Pity it wasn't on the ox's head.'

The bus was off again and soon trundling over a beautiful bridge with elegant lamps spaced along it.

'Magdalen Bridge,' her companion said. 'You should see it later in the year when the punts are out. Not long now till your stop.'

'I hope you get on well at your appointment,' Jill said to him, 'and thanks for all your help.'

Suddenly Jill felt as though a weight had lifted from her. The elderly man had helped put things into perspective. She might be a wreck but she was going to her best friend's wedding anyway. It was going to be a happy day, whatever the weather, and however scruffy she looked. Perhaps Oxford was working its charm on her, as Laura always said it would.

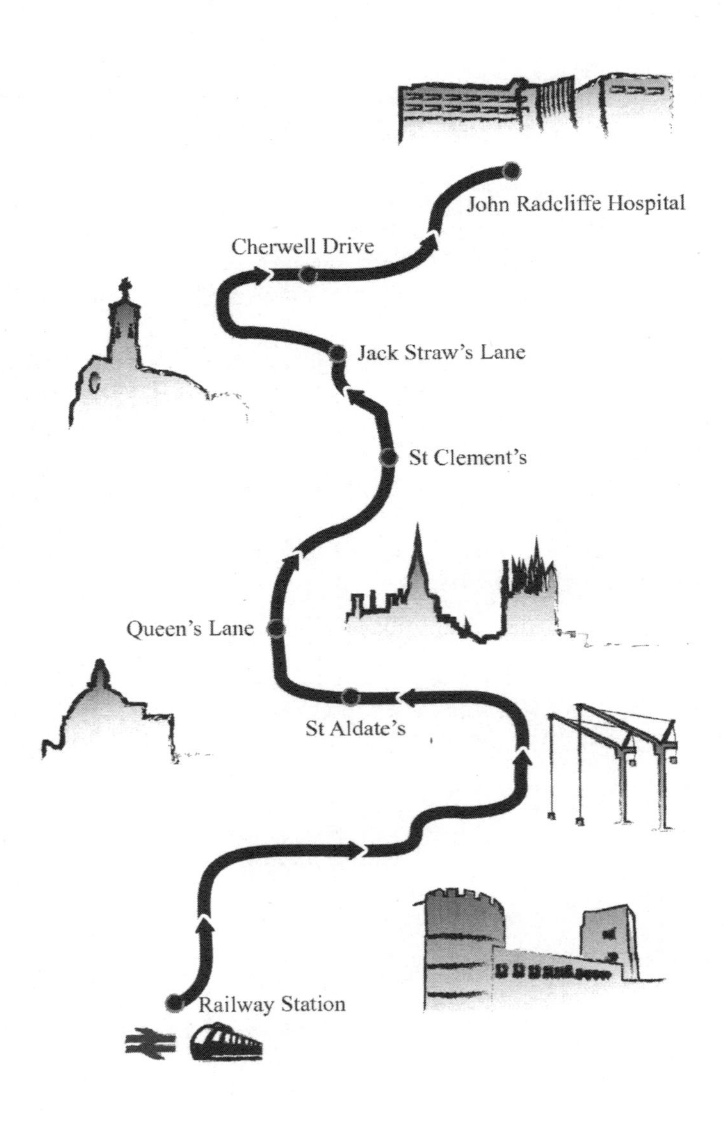
John Radcliffe Hospital
Cherwell Drive
Jack Straw's Lane
St Clement's
Queen's Lane
St Aldate's
Railway Station

Lucky in Love

CAROL MACFIE LANGE

He could feel the rhythmic thudding of his heart as the train pulled into the station. He glanced nervously at his watch. Damn! Just two minutes to spare. Would he be in time to catch the No 13 at 1.15? Janis would be waiting for the bus as usual at St Aldate's. It had started raining again, great blobs of glistening tears whipped against the window by the April winds. What if he wasn't on the bus when it reached St Aldate's? He felt the familiar, tingling unease spreading across his chest, knew that it could escalate to a debilitating anxiety, and willed himself to focus on his plan of action.

He made the journey twice weekly to visit his wife in hospital. The trips had been uneventful over two years until he met Janis. He was lonely. His need for understanding and warmth was profound. Filled with anticipation and longing, he sat like an automaton, dipping occasionally into his pocket copy of *Candide* to calm himself.

He leapt from the train before it had barely stopped, saw the No 13 still waiting, revving, rushed towards it, tripped, almost fell, righted himself and rapped red faced on the closed door.

'Come on then mate, we 'aven't got all day!' the driver yelled.

'Sorry… sorry,' Aleck muttered, fumbling for change. He paid the driver and stumbled to the middle of the bus. Left hand side, aisle seat. Janis was very specific about that. He realized he'd been holding his breath and forced himself to inhale and exhale deeply. Quickly he placed his briefcase next to him and took out several papers and a pen, spreading them carefully on the empty seat.

It was a minute before he realized his mistake. This wasn't the eighth seat on the left, it was the ninth! Before he had time to gather his things and move, a woman had bustled in from the front and ensconced herself in front of him. He stared at the bright headscarf of the woman in front of him, noticed wisps of fair hair escaping from the sides of the scarf, and as she turned to gaze out of the window, he saw that her skin was smooth and slightly pink from the wind, her small, straight nose moist and red. She took out a handkerchief and blew her nose.

He didn't want to draw attention to himself by asking her to switch seats. And yet…

'Be sure not to let anybody sit next to you,' Janis had warned often. 'Otherwise…'

'Otherwise what?'

'You know…' she'd whispered, moving her hand.

'Ah. Indeed.'

'Well then.'

Aleck shuddered. What was he to do? There wasn't anybody next to him, but he was in the wrong seat. Surely she wouldn't hold that against him? It wasn't his fault the train was late.

The tousled head in front of him shed its headscarf, shook it. A smattering of water touched the papers on the seat. The woman shook her fair hair, flexed her small red umbrella open, shook it, closed it. Aleck gazed at his papers, damp now from the spattering shower of raindrops.

'Do you mind, madam!' he grunted, irritated.

The woman turned. Her large feline eyes fixed him enquiringly, appraisingly.

'Do I mind what? The rain? No, not a bit of it. "If the rain shall make the roses bloom, then why lament its fall", etcetera, don't you think?'

'My thought exactly,' Aleck lied. The woman smiled and turned away. He was delighted, astonished. The candid merriment of her look had completely disarmed him. Where had this miraculous creature appeared from? He had never seen her on the bus before. He glanced over the seat and saw without surprise that she was holding a copy of *Candide*. It seemed mysterious, yet inexplicably natural, that they should share the same love of literature. He wondered how far she was going and when she was getting off. The thought of her getting off appalled him. He couldn't allow it. She could not get off until they had made contact.

Contact. The word brought back to him the full force of his two-year affair with Janis. He trembled at the memory of their first meeting. He had been desperately lonely in his flat in London, his wife ill in the Radcliffe, and had looked forward to the journeys with heightened anticipation of some kind of respite from the woeful circumstances of his life. His days were a series of forays into loneliness, ever deeper and more dismaying, crammed with the minutiae of senseless existence. Even his job teaching English at the college had become routine, the initial surge of exhilaration at sharing his passion for literature, his rapport with the students, all gone. Lost. Life had become something to move through stolidly and without courage, savouring nothing, but tasting daily all the bitterness of his own fate.

Janis changed all that. He looked forward to his journeys to Oxford with a kind of quivering hope. Even after his wife died, he continued the journeys. He was addicted to the ritual and the comfort of a known touch.

The first time, she had sat down without looking at him, jacket spread over her knees. She sighed, closed her eyes, her left hand softly at her side, waiting. They sat in silence. Just as the bus reached the Radcliffe, she flipped her jacket nonchalantly over his lap, moved her hand and stroked his thigh. Then she got up without a word and left the bus, leaving him rigid with bewilderment and desire.

They met regularly after that. They exchanged few words and he was uncertain of her purpose. She never looked at him. His bewilderment increased each time as she throbbed under his hand and left, aloof and silent.

She refused to see him outside of the journeys. Had commitments, she said. He saw that this was an adventure for her, a way to alleviate something unspoken in her life, and he had to accept that. He would flop down in the same seat, move over when she would come in at St Aldate's, throwing her coat with seeming carelessness across their laps. He made the remaining journey to the Radcliffe in a haze of anticipation and anxiety. Sometimes she would snatch her hand away, pick up her phone, dial his number. She manipulated him with shameless cold brutality.

'Stroke my hand,' the text might command; or, 'If you don't liven up within ten seconds, I'm leaving,' or, 'Haven't you any imagination?' and so on.

He would tremble under her hand, try to fulfil her demands, full of remorse and dread. Once he answered her text.

'I'm trying,' he typed.

'If you ever text my phone again it will be the last time,' she hissed, and placed her hand on his thigh. He succumbed.

Once she inexplicably snatched her hand away. Contrite, he placed his hand on her thigh, stroking her with soft, small movements. She moved closer. Breaking the rules, he stole a look at her. She was staring straight ahead, face rigid with concentration, a tiny flick of her upper lip the only sign of emotion. He thought she looked like the Sphinx, distant and cold. Yet his need for her touch and approval increased with each passing week.

Back in London, thinking of her in the passionless chill of his empty flat, he fantasized her in a tremulous embrace, warm and giving, and in this elevated state, broke all the rules of desire and consummation. That was the closest he ever came to Janis.

As the bus rumbled closer to St Aldate's, he caught sight of himself in the rain-slashed window, eyes bulging with anxiety, mouth a thin tight line of tension. His body felt cramped, nauseous, as if he had swallowed something he could not digest. This woman filled him with need and fear and dread. What was he doing there?

He knew what he must do. Swiftly he moved over to the window seat, crammed his briefcase under his seat and slid far down in the seat, head below the window.

The bus pulled over at St Aldate's. Nobody got off or on. He thought he could see Janis's head bobbing outside the window, trying to look in. He slid further down into the seat. The bus pulled away.

When it was safe, he sat up.

'Well done,' the woman in front said, turning, her slanted green eyes searching his amusedly. 'I thought I was going to lose you under that seat.'

'Do you mind?' he said again to the woman in front, indicating her seat.

'Not at all,' she grinned. 'Thought you'd never ask.' She moved to make a place for him.

She's beautiful, thought Aleck. Warm. Funny.

He wanted to know this woman.

'Will you join me for lunch later?' he asked.

'Funny you should say that.' She smiled at him, a broad, embracing smile that touched her merry eyes. 'I was about to say the same thing.'

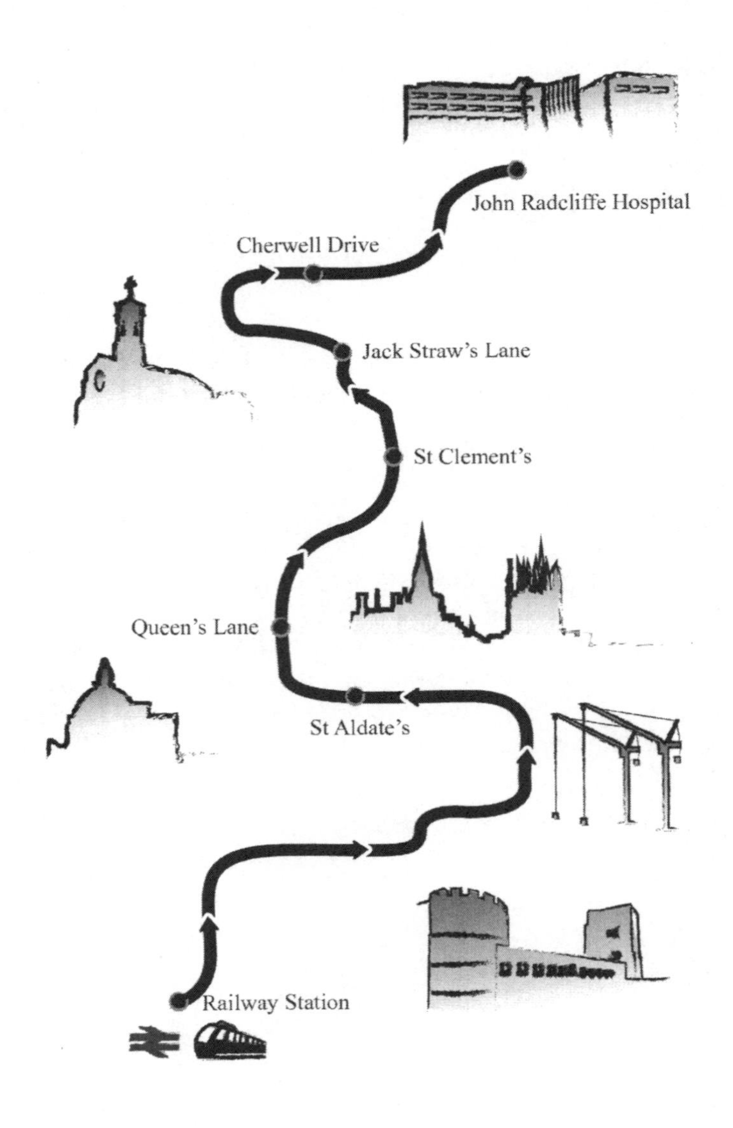
John Radcliffe Hospital
Cherwell Drive
Jack Straw's Lane
St Clement's
Queen's Lane
St Aldate's
Railway Station

Make Your Own Luck

SARAH TIPPER

Rose saw the No13 bus approach. Here it was. A shiny festive red, like holly berries. It arrived as expected at one-fifteen, and she felt relieved. She'd only got to the bus stop a minute before and she hadn't been sure if her watch was showing the right time or not. She could do with a sit down to rest her feet.

A flash of pink caught Rose's eye. On closer inspection it was a woman chasing a tiny hat. The wind was clearly keen to keep it, the woman looked desperate to retrieve it. It was woman against nature. Rose winced as the woman fell hard. For a second no one moved, the shock needed to be absorbed, and then a chap at the front of the bus queue and a teenage couple dashed over.

Rose looked at her trusty stick in one hand (a snazzy pink metal one with a floral print, quite with it and not old fashioned at all, she thought) and her sturdy hessian shopping bag in the other. She felt embarrassed on behalf of the woman in pink. Then she watched, relieved, as the woman in pink got to her feet and walked slowly towards the bus.

Rose's stomach rumbled. She was late to have her lunch. She was all at sixes and sevens today, what with shopping and now going to visit Lily. Six and seven made thirteen, she thought. She'd sit on the No13 and hope to be in less of a flap by the time she reached the hospital. She didn't want Lily to see her in a flap, she was going to offer comfort. She wouldn't mention falls or anything gloomy to Lily, not today. She had some fruit pastilles in her bag, she'd have a couple of those when she sat down.

The driver opened the bus doors and the woman in pink got on, aided by the chap who'd sprung to her assistance. Rose looked at the teenage couple who had been waiting there before her. They insisted she got on first. She thanked them. She liked to get sat down and settled before the bus moved off. She showed her pass to the driver and then got a seat by the window, one third of the way up the bus. She wasn't so decrepit yet that she needed to sit right at the front she told herself, but she preferred to stay downstairs. She was sixty-eight and she wouldn't be feeling so tired now if it hadn't been for her own foolishness in rushing round the shops.

There had been so many pretty things she'd wanted to look at that she'd forgotten her usual 'slow and steady' motto. Her granddaughter collected toy rabbits and there were plenty in the shops due to Easter. Her husband didn't like shopping in town, he said it was frenzied and crowded. He said people did it in a rush so they didn't notice how much money they were wasting. He liked shopping on the internet with a cup of tea.

The teenagers sat opposite Rose. The girl had a bright pink fringe and the boy had a blue one. Rose thought of Max Bygraves singing 'Pink Toothbrush'. Both the teenagers had black painted fingernails. She remembered when Lily's granddaughter had done that and Lily had asked her if she'd been digging in the coal?

Rose overheard the woman in pink say she was going to her best friend's wedding and felt pained, as if she herself had fallen. In the attic of Rose's mind, hidden at the back, was a dusty box marked 'best friend's wedding'. I went to the pictures with Royston before she did, thought Rose, suddenly full of teenage pique. The name Marilyn intruded into her thoughts.

She felt for her fruit pastilles. She'd have two now and that would perk her up. She knew the topmost one was green, her least favourite. What would she find underneath? She lifted the emerald sugary shape and popped it into her mouth then found blackcurrant. Bingo! Her favourite! She regarded the amethyst hued sweet with pleasure. Life was like that, you'd get the green and the purple but you had to enjoy the green too because you never knew when the purple would be coming again. She remembered a Christmas many years ago when she'd had fruit pastilles glued onto a gold painted crown to play the part of Balthazar The King in her school's nativity play. She'd liked being a king. She still thought that had been a waste of fruit pastilles though.

The back of the bus filled up. In front of Rose sat a toddler with her mum. The little girl was trying to get out of her purple coat, despite her mum's urging her to keep it on.

'Mum, why can't we go home on the train?'

'Because the train doesn't go that way.'

'Why doesn't the train go that way?'

'Because there aren't rails to our house.'

'Oh. Mum, are we having spaghetti on toast for lunch?'

'If you like.'

The child turned round in her seat and looked at Rose. Rose smiled. She received a smile in return. Rose remembered the little daily battles of what to wear and what to eat when you had a child that age.

'Amy, sit round the right way,' her Mum said.

Her Mum reached into her bag and produced the Argos catalogue.

'Why don't you look at this and you can think about what you want for your birthday.'

The bus pulled away from the train station bus stop. It stopped briefly next to the statue of the bronze ox, awaiting its turn to leave the station forecourt. Rose watched the teenage couple giggle at the ox's nether regions. Rose checked in her bag for the piece of paper she'd written on while she was talking to Lily's daughter. Rose read her neat joined-up handwriting: Lily Baker, Ward 6C. Avoid visiting at mealtimes. Nice view out of the window on the ward.

She hadn't needed to note down the view she thought. She'd been shocked that Lily was in hospital but it was only temporary. She'd be home in a day or two, before the weekend probably. She'd had a chest infection and it had sent her a bit doolally but she was on the mend. Usually Lily was as strong as the ox that had just gone out of view.

Lily Baker had met Rose Butcher when they were both thirteen. Lily's family had moved into Rose's street. They had been chums ever since. A friendship had flowered between the two young girls named after flowers. Both got married within a year of each other and had their first child in the same year. Rose glanced over at the woman in pink and remembered when she had two best friends, when she and Lily had formed two thirds of a trio. Marilyn was the first to get married. Royston was the best looking lad in their school. She shook her head imperceptibly to clear the memory, it was part shame and part jealousy, probably magnified by time into something bigger than it actually was, Rose thought, before forcing her thoughts elsewhere.

Rose thought it funny that with a surname like Baker, Lily was bad at making pastry. Rose always made extra mince pies at Christmas and took some round to Lily. Lily always made two Simnel cakes at Easter and gave one to Rose. Rose's stomach rumbled and she thought about the time she and Lily had taken the kids into town and bought doughnuts from Don Miller's. She missed their freshly baked doughnuts. She remembered her daughter with her head in the paper bag, licking up every last grain of sugar and smear of jam. She was a mucky pup.

Rose sighed, she should have gone to Nash's in the Covered Market and looked at their cakes, oh well, she was on the bus now, so it was too late. A baker's dozen is thirteen she thought. Some people didn't like the number thirteen but Rose didn't believe in bad luck, she believed in making your own luck. That's why she'd shyly asked Royston if he wanted to go to the pictures with her. Even now Rose was surprised she'd got the words out and surprised he'd said yes. Rose frowned and stuffed Royston back into the best friend's wedding box where he belonged.

Lily kept a jam jar of fortune cookie mottoes on her kitchen windowsill. If she had a Chinese take-away with the family and she got a fortune she didn't like, she'd swap it for one she did. That was Lily all over that was, she wasn't going to sit back and let life walk all over her. No, Rose wasn't worried about Lily, but she'd feel better when she'd seen her for herself.

Rose took her scarf off. She wiggled her feet in her boots. She felt restored by the sit down. She looked up at the castle mound as the bus went past. She remembered how her daughter used to like standing on the sofa and saying, 'I'm the king of the castle, you're the dirty rascal.' Rose felt that she had been a dirty rascal to Marilyn.

Rose's stomach rumbled again. She'd go to the League of Friends when she got to the hospital, it was a godsend. She'd get a cup of tea and a roll, corned beef or ham hopefully. Then she'd better go for a tinkle, and then she'd go up in the lift to see Lily. She had a *Woman's Weekly* and a copy of *The Lady* for her. Neither she nor Lily usually read *The Lady* but her at number twenty-two had passed it on. A lady admits her mistakes and apologizes thought Rose. Maybe it was time she did.

Amy looked round at Rose again.

'For my birthday I'm getting an Igglepiggle,' said Amy, pointing at the relevant page of the Argos catalogue. She kicked her legs as if her small body simply had to do something with all the excited energy this provoked.

'You are a very lucky girl. You must have been good.' Rose said.

Amy looked across at her mum, as if for confirmation.

'You've been quite good so far haven't you?' Mum said, smiling at Rose.

'Yes, I have been quite good.' Amy said, very seriously. A lot was at stake here, Igglepiggles could be taken away for bad behaviour.

'We've been to Boswells this morning,' Mum said to Rose.

'Oh, lovely. I used to take my daughter in there. She used to always want two pee to make the model train go round and she spent ages choosing marbles which she'd lose under the sofa the minute we got home.'

When the driver pulled on to St Aldate's the girl with the pink fringe sitting opposite Rose caught her eye.

'Excuse me, would you mind telling us when we get to Marston?' she asked.

'We'll be there in about fifteen minutes. I'll let you know where to get off,' replied Rose.

Rose wondered what it would be like to see the city with fresh eyes. She remembered the first solo trip she, Lily and Marilyn made into town. She thought of Selfridges, which became Allders and then Primark. She thought of Gordon Thoday, C&A, Woolworths and Littlewoods, all been and gone. The High Street was unchanged in most respects but Cornmarket Street shops were unrecognisable from her youth, apart from Boots the Chemist. No one called it Boots the Chemist now, it was just plain Boots.

Rose looked at the blossom on the tree outside St Mary the Virgin. She smiled and felt blessed. The daffodils outside Magdalen College cheered her too. The windy April day kept teasing with bright flashes of sunshine and Rose felt that spring was here at last.

The bus crawled up to the top of St Clement's. The windows had steamed up. Rose liked being on the bus when it was like this because it felt like she was out of normal time, not having to think about anything in particular, just resting and being, after the buzz of town and before the bustle of the hospital. The woman in pink got off. Rose watched her go and she thought about Lily's handbag, which contained Lily's address book, and she thought about asking for Marilyn's address and about making an overdue apology. She thought of never having to duck behind a display stand of bubble bath in Marks & Sparks again because she'd spotted Marilyn. She thought about not having to feel bad whenever anyone mentioned a friend's wedding.

Amy fidgeted again. She looked over at the pink fringed girl.

'Mum, that lady's got Barbie hair,' Amy said.

The girl smiled shyly at Amy. She was used to children commenting on her hair.

'Yes, it's nice isn't it?' Mum said.

Rose told the teenage couple when it was time to get off. Amy looked out of the bus window and waved hard at them. She began unzipping her coat.

'Leave your coat on, we're getting off in a minute,' Mum said.

Rose remembered that high intensity stage of parenting. She remembered her teenage crush on Royston. He was the sort who would have had a coloured fringe. He was probably bald now. So much of life seemed to be behind Rose. I have got a big bum, she thought, at least if I fall over I'll be cushioned. Marilyn had a big bum too, I wonder if she still has? I shan't start my letter with that though, I'll start by saying I'm sorry I didn't come to your wedding, I was just plain jealous and I dealt with it by staying away

The bus was emptier now. Rose thought about the future and how she'd help Lily out if she was at home after being in hospital but not up to her usual level of fitness. She'd offer to help make the Simnel cakes or suggest buying them instead from the Co-op. She thought about how Lily would react to being asked for Marilyn's address, having made small attempts at reconciliation between Rose and Marilyn over the years. By the time Rose got off the bus she had Spring in her voice as she departed with a wave and a cheery, 'Thank you driver.'

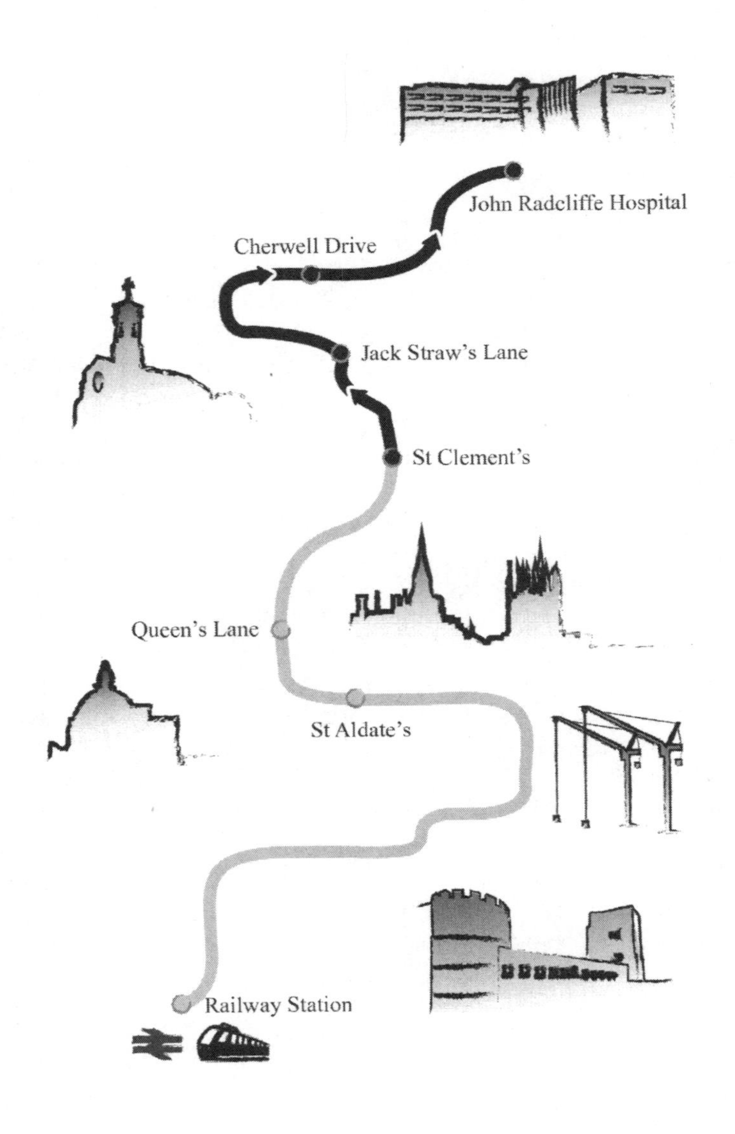
John Radcliffe Hospital
Cherwell Drive
Jack Straw's Lane
St Clement's
Queen's Lane
St Aldate's
Railway Station

Expecting

ANNA CARR

They couldn't sit together, all three of them. The two women got onto the bus first, stepping on board from the shelter outside the Thai restaurant near St Clements, walking straight past the driver towards the back of the bus.

The older woman, blonde and elegant, slid into one of a vacant pair of seats on the left. The pregnant woman who followed walked more slowly. Her canvas tote bag hit the bench seats as she swayed past them. She looked at the vacant place beside the poised woman then continued her progress up the bus, sitting in another empty seat slightly further back.

The man got on last, the doors hissing closed behind him. He tried to pay for three tickets with a twenty-pound note then fumbled change out of the pocket of his jeans. A pound coin dropped to the ridged floor and rolled away. He stamped on it with a desert boot and bent to pick it up then scanned the bus seats for the women he was with. One on the left as he looked, two thirds of the way down the bus. The other further back. Each had a spare seat next to her. He glanced over at the pregnant woman, made eye contact with her, raised an eyebrow perhaps in apology and folded himself into the space beside the blonde woman.

'I still think we could have driven,' she said as he settled into the seat next to her. 'There must be parking for patients, it's a hospital for goodness' sake.'

'Caroline, the appointment letter said to take public transport.' The man's voice was quieter than hers. He spoke slowly with a faint American accent.

'So if everyone else is getting the bloody bus there would be space for us to park.' She had a clear voice, used to making itself heard at the back of large spaces. 'This is just ghastly, Mark. Who travels on these things?'

'I always got the bus to college,' said the younger woman from behind them. 'Not this bus, the Uni one, it went straight there. We weren't allowed to park at college either.'

The older couple turned to look at her as she spoke. Mark was smiling, a little one-sided tilt to his mouth. Caroline wasn't. Her Baltic stare moved back across the gangway to the young woman's enormous pregnancy bump, her glossy brown hair, her glowing skin.

'Megan, why don't you come and sit closer to us?' Mark gestured to a vacant seat directly in front of them. The pregnant woman stood, took a step towards them. The bus moved off from the traffic lights and swung left into Marston Road. Megan swayed then tipped slightly, her pregnant belly touching the man's shoulder as she passed. He froze. Beside him, Caroline inhaled sharply and turned her head to look out of the window. She stared into the graveyard they were passing as Megan sat in front of them, extended her legs, leaning on the back of the seat so she was looking straight at Mark.

'How are you anyway?' he asked her. 'It's been ages since you told us about one of your hospital appointments.'

'Fine, thanks.' Megan's voice sounded a little croaky, almost breathless. She looked up at Mark, into his dark brown eyes. 'I don't know why the doctors keep wanting to see me, I feel fine, mostly.'

'What about the baby?' Caroline snapped her attention away from the passing cars and buildings. 'It's the baby they're worried about isn't it? That's what all this is for. That's why Mark and I are here. Why I agreed to be here.'

'Baby feels OK,' Megan said. She kept her gaze on Mark, taking in his dark eyes and full mouth. His hand on the metal back of her own seat. He shifted a little, flexing his fingers. Megan's chest went tight. Not enough air for her to breathe, just for a moment. She looked away, out of the bus window to the student halls they were passing.

'I used to live there,' she said.

'Did you?' asked Mark. 'In your first year?'

'Yes. It was fun, lots of partying.'

They fell silent. Mark shifted in his seat again, his long thigh pressing a little against Caroline's slender leg. Caroline pressed closer to him, just a little. Hip, thigh, flank touching. They were close enough for her to be aware of the smell of his deodorant, overlaid with coffee on his breath and last night's Indian food on his jacket.

She moved away again, widening the distance between them.

'Did you go to Uni, Caroline?' asked Megan.

Caroline's eyes narrowed slightly, her brow creasing into a faint frown. As if Megan had asked something incomprehensible. *Do you breathe, Caroline? Do you walk on your feet?*

'I read law at Cambridge,' she said. 'I would have thought my husband would have told you that much about me at least.'

'Oh!' Megan's eyes grew round. 'Are you a lawyer then? Like on 'The Good Wife' or something?'

'Not really.'

Mark's half smile twitched slightly. He put his hand on his wife's knee. 'Caro doesn't watch TV dramas. I doubt she's seen 'The Good Wife', have you, sweets?'

'No.'

The silence grew. Megan looked around, awkward in the quietness. 'So are you a lawyer?' she tried again.

'I'm an academic. Like my husband.'

'Really? I never saw you when I was at Uni,' said Megan. 'Mark was always coming to the bar with us and things, weren't you? I'm surprised I didn't meet you too.'

'Mmm,' Mark looked away from Megan, studying the notices on the bus walls.

'There's a bus that goes all the way to Cambridge,' he said.

'I'd like to go back there,' said Caroline. 'Maybe when the baby is here, we could take her. It's lovely there in summer.'

Megan's face twisted as if she had a sudden pain. She inhaled deeply, put her hand across her belly. The child inside wriggled and kicked in response to her.

The bus was approaching Jack Straw's Lane. Megan looked across the grassy field at the imposing bulk of an old school building. 'That's part of the Uni isn't it?' She asked.

No one answered. They sat in silence while the bus bore left, away from the main road. Caroline frowned. 'Isn't the hospital up the hill? Why are we going this way?'

'The bus goes round by some houses first,' said Mark.

'Oh for Christ's sake, we could have walked there by now,' Caroline's voice had risen in pitch and volume again.

'I can't walk that far these days,' said Megan. 'My hips hurt and the baby is heavy.'

'I thought pregnant women needed exercise?' said Caroline. 'Perhaps you wouldn't have pre-eclampsia if you had eaten and exercised properly as we asked you to.'

'It's nothing to do with it,' said Megan. 'The consultant said so last time. It's not my fault, and it's me who is in danger from it. They said I could have a fit or a stroke or something. I could die.' She looked back at Mark. 'I know this isn't how it's usually done,' she continued. 'I know I've only met Mark before but I thought we could all be friends now,' she looked towards him again, trying to meet his eyes, searching for any sign of concern for her as well as the baby she was carrying.

He just looked awkward, like someone's dad tapping his foot in a nightclub. His mouth looked petulant rather than sensuous. The smell of coffee and old curry wafting off him was making her feel sicker. The headache that had been bothering her all week was getting worse.

The baby kicked again. 'I could change my mind,' she said.

Caroline's icy gaze focussed on her again. 'No you can't.'

'Legally I can. Legally this baby is mine until I say otherwise. Perhaps I don't want it to go to Cambridge in the summer with you, it can come and live in Daventry with me instead.'

'No, she can't,' Caroline leant forward, poked Megan's soft arm with a subtly manicured fingernail. 'This is our baby. The baby you are being paid to have for us. You are just an incubator, and frankly not a very satisfactory one. You know that you've probably disadvantaged our daughter by gaining so much weight and not exercising. She is suffocating in all that flab because you can't nourish her properly.'

'It's my baby.' Megan's face flushed hot, her eyes stung with tears. The ache in her head grew worse.

'Please,' Mark looked from one to the other. 'We're nearly there now.'

'Nearly where?' asked Caroline. 'Nearly at the hospital for this stupid girl's appointment, on this bloody masochistic bus ride of yours? Nearly at our baby's birth? Nearly in court to fight for her? Nearly where exactly, Mark?'

'She is our baby,' he said, but he looked at both women.

'She's your baby,' said Megan.

'I think we can all agree on that at least,' said Caroline.

Megan turned to face forward, leant her head against the cool window. It eased the pounding just a little. She tried to sniff quietly, so the couple behind her wouldn't know she was crying. They drove through the quiet streets, not stopping to let people on or off. The bus stops were deserted.

Behind her, Mark reached for his wife's hand.

'Don't,' she said. 'Just... don't.'

They were silent as the blue and white hospital sign slid past, the bright new Children's Hospital ahead of them and the older, plainer Women's Centre at the top of the hill. Around them, cars turned and queued. Other buses waited, accelerated, stopped again. It seemed to take a long time to get through the hospital grounds to the end of the line, the bus stop outside the maternity centre, the afternoon's decisions.

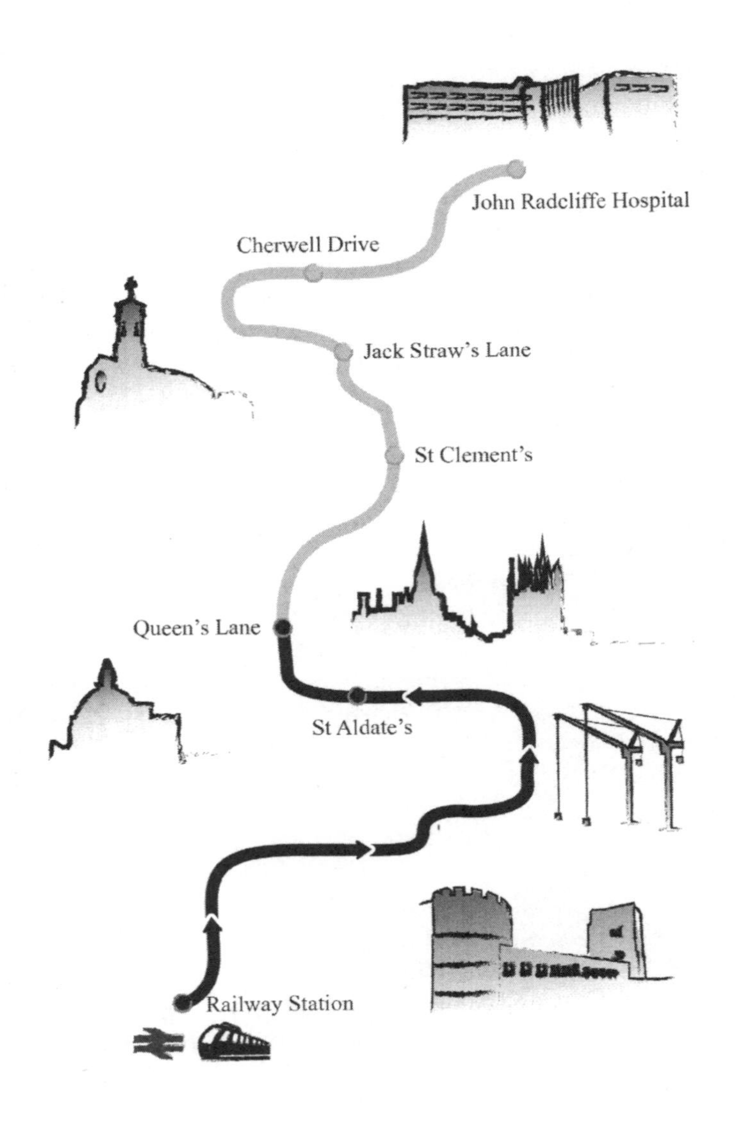
John Radcliffe Hospital
Cherwell Drive
Jack Straw's Lane
St Clement's
Queen's Lane
St Aldate's
Railway Station

The Wrong Face

JESSICA WOODWARD

The buses sat huffing and hissing while travellers poured out of the station into the blustery April sunshine. One of the travellers was Hector. Even at the age of seventy, he had a strapping walk. He descended the steps with minimal effort and gazed around him at the solemn Business School, the fuming vehicles, and the sturdy statue of an ox which somebody in a festive mood seemed to have adorned with a pink headband. His dark brown, possibly artificial hair ruffled in the wind. His eye caught the No 13 bus and he strode towards it, whipping a black leather wallet out of his suit pocket.

As he queued to board, a movement in the window of the top deck elicited a glance of interest from him, mainly because it suggested a female presence. Some dark hair swished and a red-clad elbow drooped from the window to attend to a mobile phone. Shiny, groomed nails were just about visible on a delicate hand. Hector approved of this, but could not observe it for longer, because his turn came to purchase his ticket to Queen's Lane.

He would have aimed for a top-deck seat, but he was one of the final passengers to board and the driver was anxious not to lose time. Since forward propulsion makes the stairs of a bus precarious, he remained at the lower level and took a seat next to a round, nervous-looking man of approximately his own age.

Hector was a sociable person and he cared a lot about appearance. Both of these attributes encouraged him to speak when he observed that the person next to him was wearing an Oxford college tie.

'Ah... another college man!'

The fellow passenger blushed and frowned. 'Yes...' was his reluctant reply.

'Which college? No, let me guess... Balliol!'

'It's Merton, actually.'

'Ah. The cleverest college, so they say! What did you study?'

'History.'

'No way! You don't say!'

The man gazed at him in red-faced perplexity.

'I studied History too,' continued Hector. 'At Queen's. Hector Burrows - pleasure to meet you.' He offered his hand to be shaken.

'Ivan Lurkle '.

'Ivan – Ivan Lurkle? Surely not! Are you the Ivan Lurkle who writes about the Tudors?'

'Yes. That's me.'

'Well, this is marvellous! You know, I really admire your work. And you're so fortunate to be in academia. I have a passion for the Tudor dynasty. I would have liked to undertake graduate study, but, alas, it wasn't to be.'

'That's a shame. Can I ask why?'

'Ah, well...' Hector gave a rueful chuckle. 'Let's just say the results... I got a third-class degree, you see.'

'Ah, yes – that's often a barrier.'

'They said I lacked flair, that I wrote a lot. But you, well, you obviously have flair. Bags of flair. You are lucky. You know, I would love to discuss the Tudors with you. If I may – if it's not too forward – can we exchange contact details?'

'Of – of course.'

The bus sat puffing dutifully in a line of traffic while the two men wrote down each other's telephone numbers. As it began to edge forward, Hector, sensing that Ivan was not in the frame of mind to begin an intellectual exchange immediately, embarked on another topic of conversation.

'Goodness, Oxford does look different. It's almost fifty years since I last came here. Finally managing to attend a college reunion today. The Alumni Spring Garden Party.'

'I'm going to a reunion too,' replied Ivan, a note of wistfulness entering his voice.

Hector waited for more information, but none came. He continued, 'I think we'll pass Christ Church in a minute. I should have gone to Christ Church, really, what with the Henry VIII connection. You see, I may not be good at getting a degree, but I am good at getting married. I've had six wives, like Henry. Just been through my fifth divorce, but it was completely amicable. All my divorces are amicable. We're sensible about it, we know when it's time to move on. I'm still in touch with all my wives, apart from poor Olga, of course. My third - she was poisoned by an unsavoury piece of halloumi on holiday in Greece. Poor woman. But all the others - Yolanda, Victoria, Natasha, Nessa and Ermintrude - we're still in touch. Not many men can say that.'

'I can't say that,' murmured Ivan.

'Ah, can't you? Have you had a difficult break-up?'

'I've actually never been married.'

'Oh, well. Makes life simpler, doesn't it?'

Ivan winced at the note of superiority in Hector's voice. 'If you want to know, I nearly got married to someone at Merton. She's on the list of people attending the reunion today. In the end, she found a husband who was more to her taste, as did all my classmates, as far as I'm aware. Academia won't mean much to them anymore, it'll be all about who's espoused to whom and their families and grandchildren. You think you know about feeling inadequate; this is the first time I've made it this far for a reunion. Five years ago I turned back at Oxford Station. Ten years ago I didn't even get on the train. Before that I never bought a ticket. Not everyone is star-struck by degrees, Hector. There are other things that some people prefer.'

As he finished this sentence, he turned and raised his eyebrows at Hector, who stared at him with widened, softened eyes. Further conversation was curtailed by the need to press the red 'STOP' button; they were approaching Queen's Lane. With an exclamation of, 'Your stop too, I assume!' Hector led the way down the aisle and the two of them stepped out onto the paving beside the imperial domes and pillars of Queen's.

Ivan reached out a doleful hand to part with his new acquaintance, but instead of taking it, Hector's expression broke into a dastardly grin.

'You know, the way I see it,' he remarked, 'is that each of us is very envious of what the other has - am I right?'

Ivan pondered, then gave a resigned nod.

'Well, why don't we make these reunions fun? Why don't we have a lark instead of caving in to tiresome expectations? I could be a serious Tudor scholar and you could have six wives. Do you see what I mean? We can swap and be what we always wanted to be!'

Ivan stared. He wondered if Hector might be mad and if that was why he had failed to retain his wives, but then a personal memory slid into his mind. He remembered a certain Yvonne at Merton telling him he was the most boring person she had ever met and that she did not want to stay with someone who never said or did anything interesting. His pride prickled. A combination of wanting to prove her wrong and not wanting to see her again in case he accidentally proved her right made him agree to Hector's proposition.

Hector guffawed, patted him on the shoulder and gave him a hearty shake of the hand. 'Off you go, then,' he exclaimed. 'Enjoy talking about your six wives. Say whatever you like - they won't be there to complain! Some Mertonians are going to think I'm an academic, goodness me! Call me tonight and let me know how you get on!'

With almost a skip, he headed across the High Street and towards the cobbles of Merton Street. Ivan watched him disappear, then took a deep breath and turned towards Queen's.

Unseen by both Ivan and Hector, a woman in a red cardigan and blue jeans had alighted from the top deck of the bus and observed them intently while pretending to photograph the college with her mobile phone. When Hector left, she approached Ivan.

'I'm so sorry, Ivan,' she whispered. 'It just keeps getting more bizarre.'

Ivan turned and the sight of her caused him to blush deeply. She had not changed much. Her expression was the same one of weary discontent, her hair was in the same wavy style (even if the dark colour had a dyed look to it), and her hands were as well-groomed as ever. Ivan struggled to know what to say.

'Y–Yvonne,' he finally managed to stammer. 'How are you? I heard you... I heard you got married.'

'Oh, Ivan,' she murmured, rolling her eyes. 'I certainly did. And he means well, he does mean well, but now I'm not so sure about the benefits of life being "interesting". You know, I have regretted the things I said to you. What I wouldn't give sometimes for a simpler existence. I hope we can put the past behind us and be friends?'

Ivan stared and reddened. His old feelings for Yvonne were flooding back and he was most happy to forgive her, but before he could formulate a reply, she spoke again.

'Ivan, I'm married to Hector.'

The shock released Ivan's voice. 'Oh! I see! You mean... you're the seventh? I mean to say, the six he told me about, the ones he divorced or lost, none of them were called Yvonne.'

'They were.'

'I... I don't understand.'

'They were all me, Ivan! Yolanda, Victoria, Olga, Natasha, Nessa and Ermintrude - do you see? It spells Yvonne! I'm his only wife. It's all because his degree result destroyed him. Did he tell you he wasn't good at getting a degree but he was good at getting married?'

'Yes.'

'Someone apparently said something along those lines after the result came out, to comfort him, make him think he would succeed in other spheres of life. He was a handsome young man, after all, and very popular. The idea stuck.'

'So... you mean...?'

'The more he thought about the failure of his academic dream, the more he became convinced that he was destined not to study Henry, but to carry on his legacy. A few years after we got married, he suddenly told me that it was time for him to woo his second wife. I panicked, of course, but he's not a fickle sort. He was just desperate for the superior academics in his imagination to think he was good at something. Goodness, it's a constant strain for me to stop people finding out just how far he's gone. Any chance he gets, he'll start boasting about his six successful marriages, when the reality is it's all me playing different characters at home. Oh Ivan, it is a difficult life!'

Ivan's voice was once again constrained. All he could think of to stutter was, 'But – but one of them died.'

'Olga had to die because she was the third,' returned Yvonne with a bitter laugh. 'Henry's third wife died from illness. Hector did want to mirror the fate of at least one wife, and as chopping heads off and banishing to distant castles is generally frowned upon nowadays, we agreed it would be that one. And, obviously, three is a sensitive number for Hector. Once I'd finished the halloumi, she was gone. The others come back now and again when he misses them, but we never resurrect her.'

Ivan gazed. 'I'm so sorry, Yvonne. I – I would never have imagined it. It sounds awful. '

'Well, it helps him stay more positive, but it's not easy. Anyway, what do we do? You've distracted him from the Queen's reunion, which is what I come to do every five years, as it would be so terribly embarrassing. But he didn't need me this time, he met you. What now, though? Do we fetch him from Merton? Did you really think people would believe the trick? Or that the Queen's alumni wouldn't wonder why you're wearing a Merton tie?'

A small, buried, hopeful part of Ivan had been surfacing throughout this conversation, wondering if he had been too hasty to characterise his former classmates. Yvonne seemed genuinely pleased to see him. If he could be on better terms with her, he wondered, absent-mindedly clutching his tie, perhaps he should not have spurned all the married Mertonians so soon. What if Hector was making a fool of them both, when the reconciliation could have been a success? However, he knew that Hector would not be at all keen on a change in plans.

The former couple walked along Merton Street to a black wrought-iron gate that admitted them into Christ Church Meadows. Tottering on tiptoes, they peered over the wall of Merton's garden for signs of Hector. Knots of smiling, exclaiming people with vaguely recognisable features were scattered across the lawn, but it was not until they heard a cry of, 'I never knew that about Anne of Cleves!' that they managed to locate him. Ivan's heart gave a pang. Hector's face was illuminated with the exhilaration of having his academic views heard. His audience were smiling, and while they did all seem to be wearing wedding rings, there was not a hint of the smug piety Ivan had pictured to himself. It was clear he was welcome.

'I can't believe it. They *do* think it's you!' smirked Yvonne.

Ivan made his decision. 'It's all right. I'm happy with that. Hector deserves a chance to live out his dream. And – and I'd like to tell you that it's you I've missed more than anyone since we left here.'

Yvonne turned and gazed at him in joy.

The Alumni Office at Merton were delighted to find such an eager event guest in Ivan Lurkle. Not only did he grace the Class of 1966 Garden Tea to the point of being the last to leave, he also returned for every alumni event afterwards for the rest of his life. He was so fond and supportive of the college that they made exceptions to allow him to come to the Young Alumni Get-Together and the Alumni Science Weekend, despite his not being young or scientific. Once they had updated his contact details, they telephoned to invite him to speak at the Alumni History Conference and found his enthusiasm so thunderous that a new phone had to be bought afterwards.

He took the podium in Merton's shadowy seminar room and gave a presentation on the Boleyn family that all the attendees agreed was most stimulating. With a mind so rooted in the intricacies of the past, however, it was not to be expected that he would have much focus left for the formalities of the present. Kindly chuckles rippled through the room as he began his acknowledgements by thanking his friend Ivan for writing the presentation, before hurriedly correcting himself and asserting that *he*, of course, was Ivan.

The room was dusky but the afternoon outside was bright, and at one of the outdoor cafe tables on Broad Street, a pair of old friends could be seen exclaiming at a wonderful piece of news. 'This morning, he said he'd call me Yvonne now!' may not sound world-changing to outsiders, but to Ivan, his college sweetheart's gratitude for Hector's gradual recovery was compensation for a lifetime of regret.

oxford

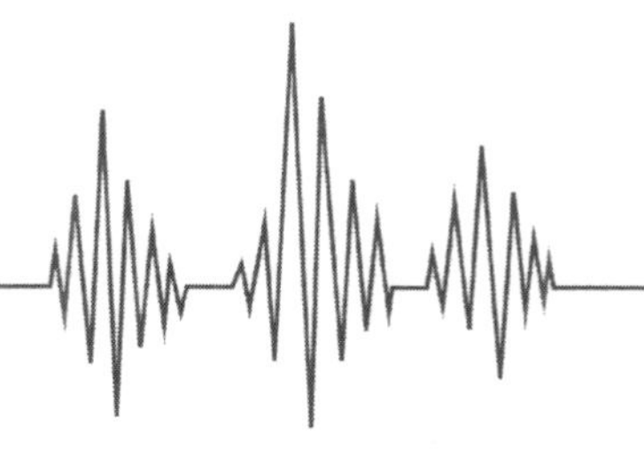

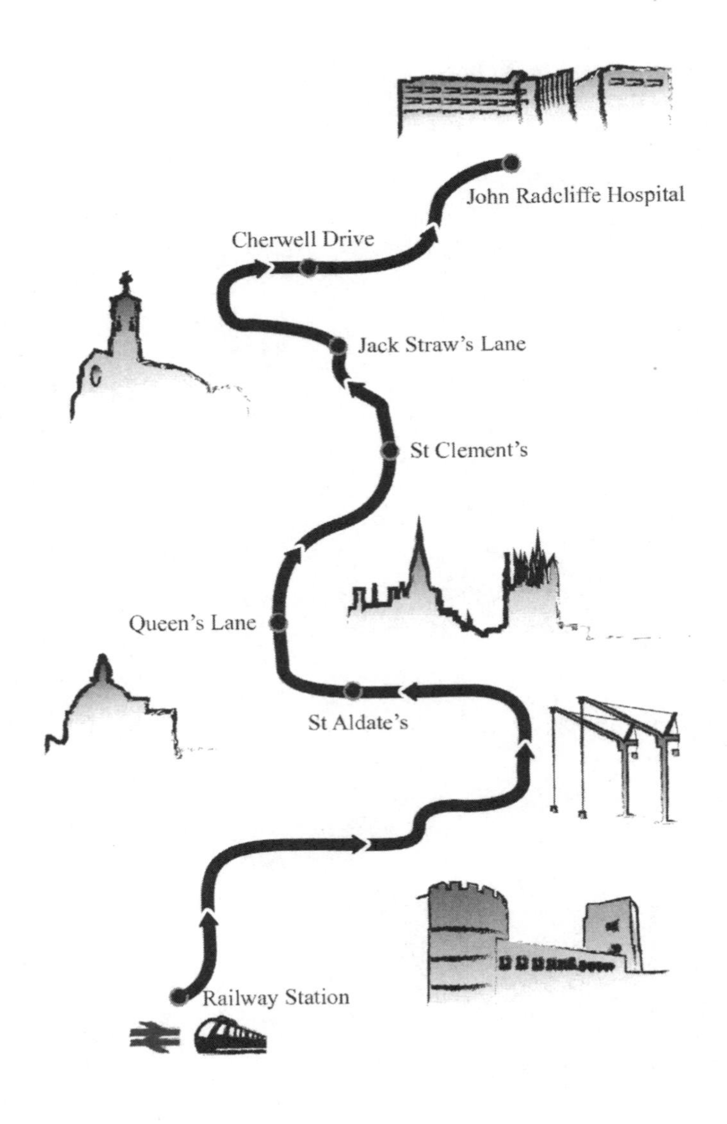
John Radcliffe Hospital
Cherwell Drive
Jack Straw's Lane
St Clement's
Queen's Lane
St Aldate's
Railway Station

The Guilt Trip

ROGER B MARSHALL

The moment she saw the post on Facebook, Stephanie knew there was no alternative: she would have to go to him. Even now, after an interval of more than twenty years, she felt the emotions of the past washing over her in great waves as she stared at the screen, sensed the adrenaline rushes of love and loss, submission and betrayal, meeting and parting. Isn't time supposed to be the healer? Why then did she feel the tug stronger now than ever before. She would have to go back to Oxford where it had all started, where they had met.

She was studying English at Wadham while Peter was a mathematician at Magdalene: in theory they might never have met, but two colliding punts and friends in common threw them together. Their meeting was both wet and mere chance, their romance hot and fiery, their parting painful and complete. They both had a share in the origins of their dilemma, passion and its consequences, but she made the decisions, right or wrong, that pulled them violently apart. Could she now find the courage to face him again, to dig that deep? You can wash your hands as often as you like but your conscience always makes the water run a little pink.

Jill's page had carried the news of Peter's illness. Jill was Peter's wife, well ex-wife, but that wasn't the point. The point was that it had been Jill who had helped Peter pick up the pieces after Stephanie left and in doing so formed a bond that led directly to their marriage. Stephanie had created the rift and the pain; Jill had helped to heal the pain, which led to the altar, which led to Anna, the daughter.

Anna was on Facebook too, and on many other social media sites. Stephanie had followed the links and kept a distant view of Anna's life to date. It wasn't hard because she was often in the public eye. What was hard was seeing Peter's eyes under those dark eyebrows. Picking out those telltale traces of his square jaw line, the lines that gave Anna such a beautiful, striking presence. Seeing that radiance which, in her indisputably biased eyes reflected only Peter's good points and nothing of Jill, nothing of note anyway. Yes, Anna had Jill's long dark hair and her elegant height, but that was trivial by comparison. On the cat walk they served only to support and frame that majestic head. There were constant reminders in the media, constant tugs at her conscience; every time she saw Anna she saw Peter. Anna was the daughter she never had.

Stephanie was nearing the end of her pilgrimage now. It had begun much earlier with the short, wet walk from home, a 131 bus into always busy Wimbledon, the District Line tube to Paddington and the smell of the railway, the train up to Oxford and now the No 13 towards the hospital. She should have become more settled and sure of herself as she neared her journey's end, but instead the fears and insecurities were winning.

'Return to the John Radcliff Hospital, please. How much is that?'

'For you my duck, three-fifty.'

'Thanks.'

You wouldn't get that on a London bus. Not a flipping word usually, certainly never a friendly word delivered with a smile.

Sitting upstairs at the front, like some bright-eyed five-year-old, she thought she could feel relaxed for the first time today, but almost immediately the doubts started to creep back into her consciousness. Number thirteen. Too many thirteens in this route for her liking. There were enough ghosts lurking about without any help from the real world. She tried to concentrate on the view. Every now and again the sun would pop out, which she took as a good sign, only for the clouds to roll over once more and pull her with their ominous power, back into one of her darker moods.

It was probably a good thing that her decision had needed to be a sudden one, made instinctively and immediately when she read the news. An hour or so of feverish searching online and planning her route and timings had been all she had allowed herself. Another hour deciding what to wear, washing her hair, working with the straighteners. If only she had slept better. If only she had been able to plan things out in a more leisurely fashion, taken time to think through what to say. If only. There were too many things in her life that she could say that about. If only I had done this. If only I hadn't done the other.

In another life, within some mathematician's dream of a parallel universe, she could have had Peter's child, Peter's daughter, her own version of Anna. In that other place she could have been Peter's wife. Then, it could have been her daughter on the front page of Vogue. There was a thirteen back then too, but the thought of it was too painful to dwell on.

Instead she had slipped away from Oxford and finished her studies at home in Esher. In a bedroom full of pink furnishings, fluffy rugs, teddy bears and silly dolls; Mummy's little girl, never to grow up. Special considerations were applied so she got her degree, though not a good one. It didn't matter. Nothing mattered at that time.

After a few weeks to allow the dust to settle, her father took an extended leave from his partnership, a firm of surveyors, and swept the three of them off to Provence for late summer and into the Autumn. At first they lived quietly in a small whitewashed cottage on the edge of a small village, walked in for bread and croissants every morning, improved their French, made friends with other escaped Brits and generally attempted to relax. Stephanie worked at a first novel. She thought at the time this was what she really wanted to do, but soon discovered that perhaps it wasn't after all. What she enjoyed most was cooking, even though food was plentiful and wonderful all around them. She changed tack and started to research local recipes, the kind that grandmas have tucked away in old diaries or only in their heads. Among the local residents she found a young Frenchman with a camera and some spare time and together they set about creating yet another slice through the glorious apple that is traditional French home cooking.

Creating a book is one thing, albeit an honourable one, but getting it published is quite another. That took huge amounts of energy and time but eventually their baby hit the bookshops and sold modestly. Since then she had travelled, delved, eaten, cooked and written her way across most of Europe, for ten years of which she was married to Jean-Claude and his camera. But somewhere along the road Jean-Claude had met Karin from Stockholm and turned left while Stephanie turned right. She had no regrets about it now. They had enjoyed their time together but probably both always knew that it had been a marriage of convenience rather than a wild dive into a pool of passion. That special kind of passion she had once enjoyed with Peter.

They never had children, though they tried. Doctors told Stephanie, when help was eventually sought, that her earlier escapades had probably caused significant damage and it was unlikely that she would conceive, and that it was even more unlikely if she did that she could bring a baby to term. Perhaps that was a factor in the departure of Jean-Claude towards that wide-hipped Scandinavian beauty.

Without him, Stephanie found increased success with radio work, a little television and yet more books. Recently, however, another facet of life without Jean-Claude had come to the fore. Attending the opening of a new restaurant in a chain with which she had been associated commercially, and without her man to drive her home, she had fallen foul of a speed trap and been taken to court. Being found to be very significantly over the limit, the experience was not just sobering and expensive, but had cost her the loss of her licence for a while. In central London this was no barrier, but longer journeys now required her to study and plan, instead of tapping in a post code and following the clear instructions of the well-informed lady who lived behind the dashboard. It had made travel more of an adventure. One good thing she had found was that she was gradually catching up on the huge number of books that had accumulated in her reading pile, in the past they had had to wait until she went on one of her hunting expeditions abroad. Buses and trains provided lots of personal reading space.

She still saw Jean-Claude from time to time. They had parted on reasonably agreeable terms, so with no children and little property to fight over it had been quite a grown-up affair, and secretly Stephanie rather liked Karin Peterson, even if she did have perfect blonde hair and child-bearing hips. It helped that she admitted that she couldn't cook to save her life. Jean-Claude was going to be a busy boy: working for a living, kids around his ankles and all the cooking to do. Well, to be fair he seemed to be coping, two children so far, and they were still together. Good luck to them both.

Would she and Peter still be together if she had stayed with him? If she had not had the termination and fled? She remembered the date because it was a date you couldn't forget, May 13th 1994. She knew it had been a girl. She had asked them, pleaded to know. She thought it would have made it better, but it only made it worse, brought back to the surface once Anna had hit the headlines. She should have stayed with Peter and had the baby, but he had flipped when she gave him the unexpected news and she became scared, she had never seen him in such a foul mood before. She got cold feet and ran for the exit.

It was unclear on Facebook how ill Peter was, but it sounded bad. It sounded very bad. She didn't even know if she would be allowed to see him, but she checked visiting times and it seemed possible, although she might have to wait until three, it depended on which ward he was in. She thought he would be in the West Wing and have quiet time from one till three. She should have been better prepared. It could be that only two visitors might be possible too, and she had no idea whether anyone else would be visiting, Jill, Anna? She wasn't family, so she might slip off the bottom of the priority list. The thoughts of a wasted journey began to dog her.

The chug-chug of the bus was calming. It was warm up there from the fifty percent of the time the sun shone in through her window. If she tried very hard to clear her mind she could almost doze, she felt her eyelids getting heavy. No sooner had she had started to feel relaxed than she saw they were coming slightly uphill towards a large modern complex. Twenty years since her days in Oxford; she had never visited the hospital then. Suddenly panic raced through her veins and she stood and turned to ask a lady sitting some way behind her, discovering that, yes, it was the JR, as they called it, and the first stop was the West Wing. She wasn't exactly sure where to go but it made sense to get off at the first stop and enquire there.

There was a queue at the desk, but everyone was very helpful and eventually she ended up in the right place and at the correct time. There was even time for a coffee and bun and time to think about what she was going to say. She wondered whether there was any mileage in doing a feature on hospital food, or food for hospital visitors. But she had a feeling it might not be exciting enough. Most of the customers had too many other things on their minds to worry about how good the cakes were. In that respect she was an unusual client.

Inside the corridors that led into the wards, the hospital became a much more serious place than the bright entrance hall and cafeteria downstairs had hinted at. Here, the smells and sounds of hard-working staff focused on mending people took over from the trivial lives of the visitors. Here lay the setting for a continual stream of life and death struggles. Here was where she was going to have to revisit a life-changing situation of their own, one which had ended sadly.

The guy sitting at the nurses' station directed her and she was finally there. He seemed to be asleep but she couldn't be sure, so she spoke anyway.

'Hello. How are you Peter?' she started, despite having carefully decided not to say that. It just came out. She was so annoyed with herself for switching to automatic. 'It's been a while, hasn't it. Can you hear me all right?'

'Yes, but I had a tube in and my voice is a bit soft.'

They stared at one another, Peter seeing her haloed by the light from the windows behind her, Stephanie seeing him smaller and strangely fragile against the pillows.

'Golly, Stephanie. Is that you? I can't believe it's really you.'

She could not believe it either, but when she concentrated to ignore the hospital setting, she found he had hardly changed. Stephanie didn't want him to try to return the unspoken compliment, because she looked in the mirror every day and knew he'd be lying if he said that. It amazed her that despite the metal-framed hospital bed and all the wires and tubes she could still see his face as it was on the day they first met, a bright chilly October day, the sun slanting through the trees over the river as the boats crashed, one riding up onto the other. They were soaked and so nearly overturned.

'Of course we've changed. It must be, oh, twenty years is it?' he managed.

Twenty years, yes, something over twenty years. She didn't need to acknowledge the truth.

'I was so worried about you, but I couldn't get in touch, all my letters came back.'

'That was my mother. She wrapped me up in a protective cocoon.'

There was a lull in the conversation while each considered what exactly had been done and by whom. She had left him and Oxford, she had decided on the termination.

She had been the destructive force. But she couldn't bring that up. It was small talk that was needed now.

'How are Jill and Anna?' she asked.

'Fine, I think, I haven't seen them for a while. We tend to fight. Look, this is the thing. I have a brain tumour, but it's benign and operable. They plan to take it out.'

'That sounds terrible, Peter, but it's good they can remove it.'

'Yes, my days were a bit black, but this is better. And now you've come too. Have a grape.'

'I hope they're organic.'

'Of course, you're a foodie these days aren't you? You know, one thing about lying in hospital, you have to keep a sense of perspective. If you can't laugh at life, you might as well just give up. What you come to realise is that all the everyday stuff is irrelevant. So, I no longer give a toss about whether something is organic or not, about eating too much red meat, having a bottle of wine. What really matters are people and love and beautiful things like sunsets and trees. And now, I might be given the chance to experience a few more. And suddenly you are here as well.'

'Yes, and I'm just as amazed about that as you are.'

I think I would quite like the idea of seeing you around when I get through with this. Are you ready for that?'

'I'm happy to give it a try. It's only been twenty years.'

Stephanie gently squeezed the hand she had been holding without realising since she had sat down next to the bed. She was still holding it when she realized that Peter had nodded off and a nurse was standing next to her.

'I think he needs to sleep, dear.' she said gently. 'He does this from time to time. Perhaps you can see him again tomorrow evening after his op.'

'Yes, that would be wonderful.'

oxford

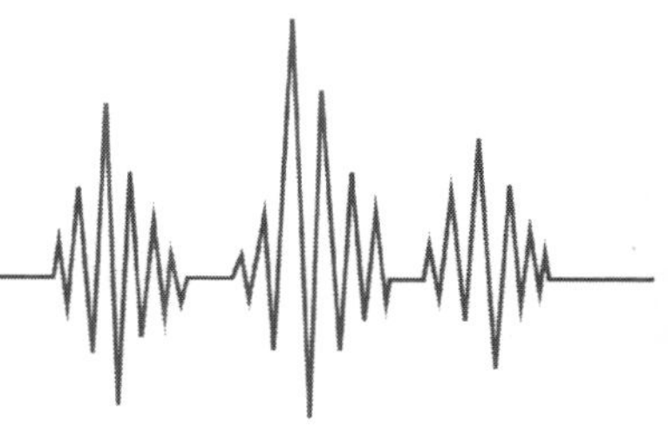

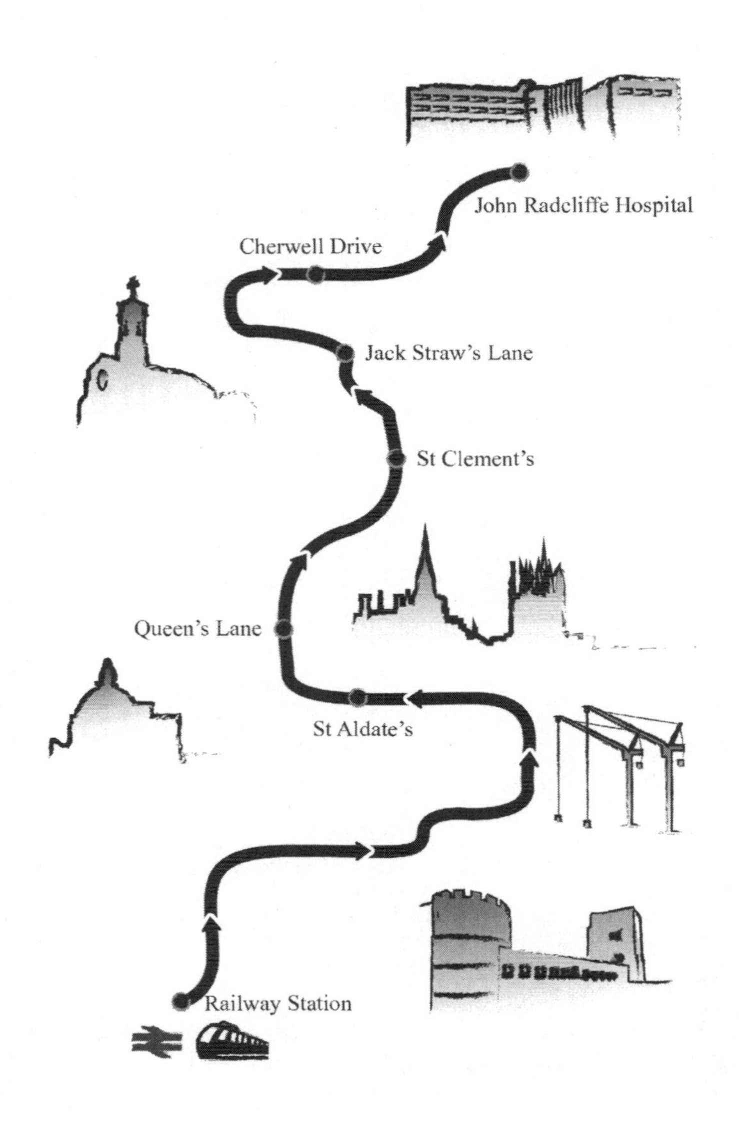
John Radcliffe Hospital
Cherwell Drive
Jack Straw's Lane
St Clement's
Queen's Lane
St Aldate's
Railway Station

Rose

PAULINE MASSEY

She came tottering down the station steps in the highest heels. Her coat was long and trailing, her lips as red as strawberry jam. She was pulling a tiny case behind her. It clattered down the steps so that others turned to look at what was causing the racket.

'Taxi! Taxi!' she called across the road, once she had reached the bottom of the steps. The taxi rank was opposite. Why didn't she just cross the road, Bernard thought, and go to the front of the queue?

He was waiting for the No 13 bus. How nice it would be to be able to afford a taxi, he thought, but he mustn't dwell on difficulties. His wife had told him to be cheerful, for a change. He hated the way she said that, as though she were sick and tired of him and his digestive issues. Retirement wasn't all it was cracked up to be when you had a wife like Sheila. Bernard smiled to himself. Well, at least he had a day off today. The woman with the heels had at last decided to teeter across the road towards the taxi rank. Now there was a woman, Bernard thought to himself. She was no spring chicken but she knew how to cut a dash. Her hair was long and lavish, streaming down her back in auburn waves. Sheila's grey locks were stringy. Bernard shuddered when he thought of them.

Bernard looked at his watch. The bus was late, probably got caught up near the Westgate. Lots of changes going on there. Sheila had said, 'Once it's all finished I expect you to take me shopping there, Bernard. Bernard – are you listening? I said once the Westgate is finished...'

He sighed. Life wasn't getting any easier with age. Then he thought of his day out and smiled again. He had been thoughtful this time; he had a bunch of roses in one hand, bought from Marks at the station. Chocolates were already in his shopping bag. It was going to be a good day. Even his digestion was under control. Strange that, whenever he had a 'day off' as he called it, his gastric juices didn't bother him.

'You tell those doctors when you get to the JR, Bernard, you just tell them, you need something doing about all that burping. Tell them your wife's getting fed up with it.'

Ah, the JR. Not a place that people usually like to visit. Hospitals are not everyone's idea of a good day out. But for Bernard it had turned out to be just his cup of tea. He laughed when he thought of it. Spilling that cuppa had proved to be just the ticket in the end.

What was happening across the road? The woman in the high heels was prancing away from the taxi rank and heading back across the road towards the bus stop.

'Is this where I get the bus to the John Radcliffe hospital?'

Bernard nodded. 'It's a bit late but then Oxford has lots going on at the moment.'

The woman tossed her auburn curls and brought her screeching suitcase to a halt. Bernard was glad about that. The noise had set his teeth on edge.

'Taxi man said there's something wrong with the engine. I can't wait for another. My appointment's just after two. He said there's a bus due any minute.'

Bernard looked at his watch. 'You should make it if the bus gets here soon.'

At that moment the big red bus hauled into view, coming round the corner and on to the station forecourt. Bernard mused that the bus was a paler shade of red than the woman's lipstick. She was wrapping her long coat around her. He could tell she was nervous.

'Here we are,' he told her cheerily.

But he could see there were tears. If anything, they enhanced the colour of her eyes which reminded him of a picture he had once seen of the Caribbean sea, aquamarine.

'You'll be all right,' he told her gently. 'They look after you well at the John Radcliffe.'

The woman sniffed. 'I hope so,' she murmured.

Bernard proffered his bus pass and went to find himself a seat. He noticed that the woman had a pensioner's pass too. Who would have thought it? At last they were underway, the bus swinging away from the station forecourt and passing 'the load of bull' outside the Said business school. Bernard giggled when he thought of their name for it. Sometimes the ox, for that's what it really was, sported scarves and knitted woollies. Pranks by the students.

The switchback ride around the Westgate building works set his heart racing. Bernard always enjoyed this bit of his day out. The anticipation, the knowledge that he was on his way to the JR, away from Sheila. One part of him was sorry. He had loved Sheila once, very much, and she had loved him. But that love had withered over the years. Bernard acknowledged that he was as much to blame as his wife. They had 'grown apart', that old cliché.

The woman in the stiletto heels was sitting across the aisle from Bernard, staring out of the window.

'Nice blossom there,' he commented, pointing to the pink blooms illuminated against the wall of Christ Church.

'It is lovely,' the woman in the heels agreed. 'Which college is that?'

'Christ Church, sometimes known as the House.' That's what a friend of Bernard's had told him anyway, someone who had worked there briefly in the lodge.

But now they were amongst the crowds in town and there was a long queue waiting to get on the No 13 in St Aldate's. The woman opposite Bernard was checking her watch.

'You'll make it on time,' Bernard said and smiled.

He knew this bus, the one-fifteen from the station. He took it quite regularly nowadays. Once again, Bernard smiled.

He was happy on his 'day off'. He had placed the roses carefully on the seat beside him. They weren't the garish red of the woman's lipstick, but a deep red, a comforting warming colour, the colour of love.

At last the bus headed towards Carfax, turning away from the crowds in Cornmarket and into the High Street. There was no less bustle here. The students had recently returned; it had been an early Easter. And tourists were already walking in large groups. At Queen's Lane the bus pulled up once more and there was a pause while the driver waited for his replacement to take over the bus.

The woman across the aisle turned to Bernard and blurted out, 'I think I'm suffering the wages of sin.' Bernard said nothing. She hesitated and then went on, 'I'm ill because I deceived my husband. And he was always good to me.'

A shudder passed through Bernard. 'That cannot be true,' he said kindly and, picking up his roses and shopping bag containing the chocolates, he went to sit next to the distraught woman. He was tempted to hold her hand. It looked white and fragile despite the long, red finger nails which he imagined could be pretty lethal if misused.

The bus had set off again and was now trundling over Magdalen Bridge and heading towards St Clement's.

'Look,' Bernard said, trying to distract his companion. 'That's where people go punting.' He pointed down to the Cherwell but the woman wasn't interested.

'It's cruel to have an affair,' she declared. 'But I couldn't help it. I just fell in love with someone else. I didn't think that would happen at my age.'

'You are very glamorous,' Bernard told her. 'I'm not surprised at all.'

The woman turned to look at Bernard for the first time. Her eyes were swimming with tears, those lovely eyes which were the colour of the sea under sunshine. Bernard thought he might drown in their depths. Then he remembered. This was his 'day off'. He was travelling to the JR to visit...

'Have you ever had an affair?' Her question was direct, her blue-green eyes penetrating.

Bernard swallowed hard. He looked out of the window to try and calm himself. The bus was already driving speedily along the Marston Road. Soon their journey would be at an end. They would arrive at the hospital.

'Yes,' he said at last, and there was anguish in his tone. 'I'm on my way to see her now. We met when I spilled a cup of tea on her lap in the League of Friends café. That's where we meet, in the League of Friends café every Wednesday. I tell my wife I'm going to the JR to see the consultant about my gastric troubles.'

Suddenly the woman was laughing. 'And you mean she falls for that story? How many of us get weekly appointments with a consultant these days?'

Bernard cleared his throat. 'I hadn't thought of that.'

'Maybe your wife enjoys your days out as much as you do.'

Bernard hadn't considered that either.

They were already at the West Wing. There was the helicopter pad, empty for now.

'You've made me feel better,' the woman said, 'my name's Rose, by the way. And I'll be in the hospital for a couple of weeks. Just in case you feel like another day out.'

Bernard smiled. Spring was in the air and nature was burgeoning. And it felt as though there was no end to life's possibilities.

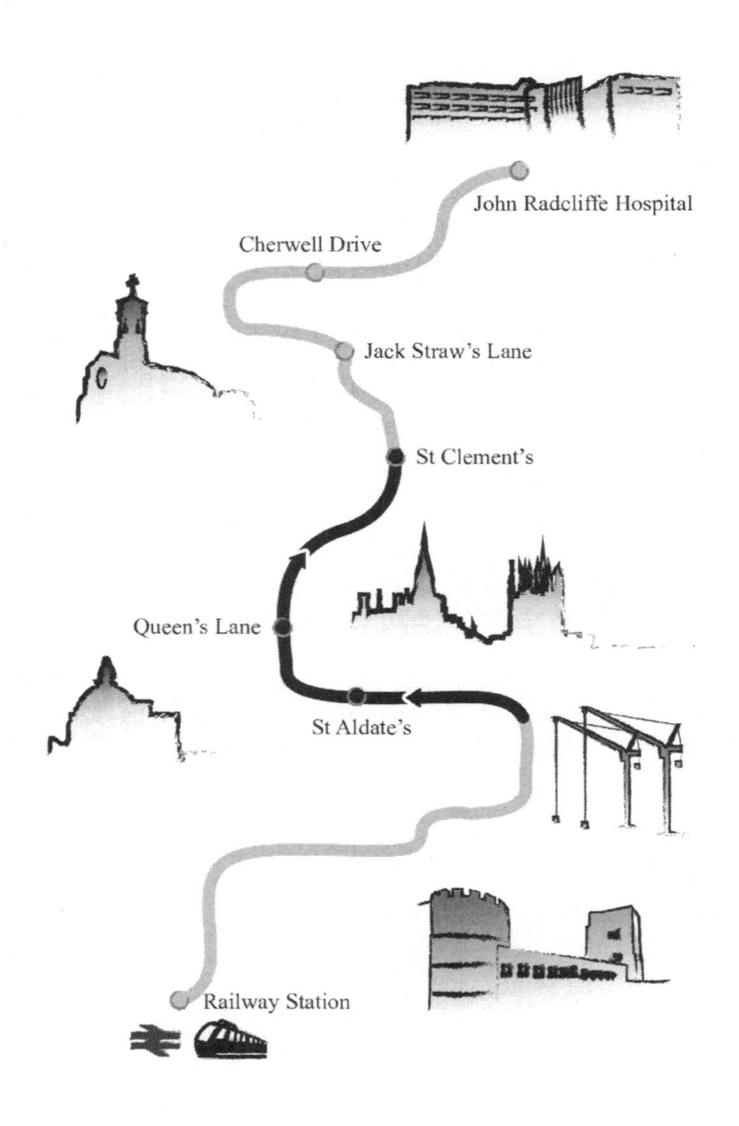
John Radcliffe Hospital
Cherwell Drive
Jack Straw's Lane
St Clement's
Queen's Lane
St Aldate's
Railway Station

Way to Go

KAREN GRAY

Wake up. Go on, you know you'v got to. Fumble a hand out from under the bedclothes and silence the alarm. Rub your eyes, wonder that you managed to sleep at all. But now that you're awake, get out of bed. Today's the day.

Switch the radio on as the kettle boils and think about why you picked this day, the one that comes round only once in four years, the 29th of February. Pause, mug in hand, as you remember the feature on the radio, the challenge to do something out of the ordinary. Feel your stomach spiral down a sink hole as you relive committing to your crazy leap-day resolution.

Just to please her, allow yourself to be fed 'a proper breakfast'.

'Come on now, love, eat up. It'll keep you going longer than those fags of yours!'

Scrambled egg on toast, two cups of strong tea. No sugar though, she won't allow it. Ease your thumb inside the waistband of your trousers. Notice how much tighter it is these days. More stomach, less hair. Regret the extra slice of toast. Pretend you're feeling fine when she asks you every five minutes. Don't let her see you biting your nails, hide the raw, peeled pinkness of your fingers in the palm of your hand as she clears away. Know that she knows but hear her say nothing. Watch as she walks stiffly into the kitchen, one hand holding your empty plate, the other pressed to her hip.

Go back to the front room to wait for your son to arrive. As you turn to lower yourself into your chair by the fireplace, your feet settle into the worn patch on the carpet. Sit and listen to the insistent ticking of the glass-domed clock on the mantelpiece and wish it didn't have to be lunchtime, although the bus might be quieter then. She's got your coat ready, your favourite one that zips up the front. The zip's broken but you don't tell her. The doorbell rings.

'Ready?'

Force a smile, stub out the cigarette and take her outstretched hand. Feel how her wedding ring cuts into her finger. It never used to.

In the street, buttressed by an arm on each side, keep your eyes down as you walk to the Speedwell Street stop. Clutch your wife's hand, get an encouraging squeeze. It's ok, you're not alone. Not yet.

At the bus stop, stand.

Wait.

The No 13 bus is coming for you. It's big. It's red. It's noisy. Stop yourself putting your hands over your ears and try not to think what red means. Don't go there…

Your wife gives you a push and nearly knocks you both off balance.

'On you get then, got your money?'

Propel yourself off the pavement and into the bus. Buy yourself a ticket. Day Return. Adult. That's you, remember. You can do this. You're heading to the back. Ease your way along the bus, past the space reserved for wheelchairs and buggies, shun the stairs to the top deck, pull yourself up one level, up another and reach the back. Turn and sink onto a seat. Press your back into it and push your hands down either side of you. The seat is solid beneath you, behind you. Give a silent cheer, you've made it this far, you're on the bus.

You're on the bus!

Look up and see the two of them standing outside on the pavement, the glass clear but hard between you. Your son smiles, runs a hand through his hair, gives you the thumbs up. He's had to ask for time off work for this, a long lunch hour; got to work late tonight to make up for it. He's been a good son. Admit it.

Your wife, the wire wool of her permed grey hair unmoved by the April breezes, gives you a wave but doesn't manage a smile. Dear God she looks drawn. Ignore that for now, think how proud she'll be if you pull this off. Not to mention all those strangers you'll never meet, out there on the airwaves, sharing your journey. They're all rooting for you. Hang on to that thought.

Brace yourself, the bus is moving off. First the milk float whine of the electric engine starting up, then the vibration of the diesel kicking in behind. You're sat right on top of it, a juddering heartbeat, just like your own. Sense the old feelings seeping back, that numbing tiredness, like your brain is on pause. Come on, you knew this would happen, drop those shoulders. Pretend you do this every day. After all, you did, back in the days when you used to work in Cowley, remember?

Think back to when your son drove you on a practice run around the route last weekend, your memories jarred by the changes: a new shop front here, a whole building vanished there. Spot the express supermarket your wife walks to each morning for her daily dose of food, news and friendship.

'I saw Ruby today, she's still under the doctor, and that daughter of hers has gone and moved in with her again. That's the third time, or is it the fourth? Don't know why she puts up with it! Sends you her love…'

Watch out! The High Street is heaving. A motorbike skids between cars, the horn of an angry driver clouts your ears, trucks and buses clog the air with diesel fumes. Through the window people mill and mingle and swarm. The glass shields you, it's clear and hard. It's ok. You're ok.

No you're not. Look away. Clutch your newspaper. Remember the plan. All you have to do is sit here as far as St Clement's, get off the bus and cross over to the pub for a quick half of Dutch courage. Down your beer and then get back on the bus in the other direction and - home. It would be easier to sit tight all the way to the JR, switch buses and come back again, but that wasn't the deal. Don't even think about it. Concentrate instead on the texts tapped in by your son to the phone he bought you.

'I'm right with you, dad, you can do this!'

Try not to let the old ways get the better of you. Distract yourself, they said. Look around at the other passengers, see what they're up to. The young chap hiding in a hoody has got his eyes closed, ears wired, head nodding. A middle aged man, checking his watch, sits by the side of an elderly woman. His mother? She looks pale, holds her handbag tight on her lap. There's a group of foreign students, four square, facing each other, chatting away. Spanish, is it? Can't understand a word but they're laughing. Wonder at their youth, their ease, the girl's neon socks. Some of the passengers look bored, they probably do this journey every day and never a second thought. It's alright for them, they're all normal. Just for a minute, allow yourself a little pinch of envy, taste the bitterness, then swallow it back down again.

Sing. Just in your head, mind, not out loud, don't draw attention to yourself. Hum the tune you danced the first dance to when you got married. She insists it was playing the day you met at that party. Thirty years ago was it? More? You were standing in the kitchen, hanging onto your pint glass, afraid it would get lost if you put it down. She was talking to your mate, you saw her throw her head back as she laughed, dark hair flying. Remember how full of life she was, close your eyes and picture that sideways look she tossed you, so sure of herself. Thank the Lord she said yes when you asked her to dance. You had no idea what song was playing but you took her word for it later when the wedding talk started, a leap of faith, just like now. Sitting on this bus because she believes in you. Don't let her down.

Open your eyes to see you're over Magdalen Bridge and nearly there. Time to move. Push the button and get up, move carefully down the bus, wait by the door behind that girl with the piercings and the pushchair, get ready to step out of the bus when the door opens and onto the pavement. Come on now, don't just sit there and imagine it all. Get up and do it!

It's colder outside. Only those few steps to the pub opposite. Drag yourself across the road, you could be wearing deep sea diver's boots for all the progress you're making. Put your hand on your chest, your heart's thudding like the spin cycle on the washing machine at home. Get as far as the bar, lean on it and run over your script in your head,

'I'll have half a bitter please.'

Say it. Ignore the way the barman looks at you when he leaves your change on the counter. Give thanks for the familiar feel of the glass in your hand, the tickle of the foam on your lips. Stop shaking, will you! You've earned this. Take a big, cool mouthful. When the last drop has gone and there's no other excuse, leave the pub and stand at the bus stop. Turn your collar up, look down the road. The homeward stretch. When the bus arrives, step inside. This time, the reds and greys look friendly, familiar. Wave your ticket at the driver and turn to the back again.

Freeze.

This bus is busier, all the seats at the back are taken. Stand there, as people push past you. One lady gives a polite, 'Excuse me!' and smiles. Let her by, avoiding her eyes, then turn round. You need to get off this bus and go back outside, to wait for the next one. Too late. The bus whines into motion, your body sways and your head swims. Fall into the nearest seat and feel your top lip break out in a sweat. Breathe. That's it, slow it down. Try to ward off that chest-crushing thing closing in on you. Know you're failing. Hear your breathing get faster and shallower, then remember the newspaper crumpled in your hand. Unfold it, peer at the headlines and feel for your glasses. Pat every pocket. Twice. Curse your absentmindedness, your damn stupidity. Look around you as the colour drains from your face and your hands start to shake. Don't lose it now.

DON'T lose it now!

Find a gentle hand on your arm and a voice in your ear, 'You can borrow mine if you like.'

Her words flow over you like cool spring water. The lady passenger tells you she does the same thing all the time. She hunts in her bag, laughs about how easy it is to lose small things in the bottom of big bags, asks where you are going and chats away when you don't answer. Focus on her voice. Look away from the fear.

Wait a minute, you're back where you started. Spot their faces at the bus stop, raise a shaky hand to the window. Your son grins and your wife searches your face. Punch the air as you stumble off. Tell them it was just fine, the beer tasted great, everything went according to plan, no problem. No problem at all. Remember the lady passenger and turn to find her, but you've missed your chance. Idiot! Wave futile thanks to the back of the bus disappearing round the bend towards the station.

Your son ushers you through the front door with a comic bow. You all laugh. Feel the welcoming hug of the house, you're elated, triumphant. Banjaxed. Start to make plans, boast about branching out, perhaps a shopping trip to the High, a meal out in that little Italian you used to go to. Why not? Sky's the limit!

Your son gives you a high five. Tell him yes, you're fine, he can go. Put your hands in your coat pockets, casual-like to prove it, and find your ticket, pull it out, the name of the bus company big and bold at the top. Run your thumb underneath the biggest, boldest word. 'OXFORD'. Is it on your doorstep, a million miles from here, or just a bus ride away?

Gaze around the front room and catch sight of the framed print of your son's graduation, pride of place on the sideboard. Your wife dusts it every day. Never misses. Tuck your ticket into the corner of the frame and stand back. Pick it up and rub the fingermarks off with your sleeve.

When your wife comes back from seeing your son out, put your arm around her. Say nothing but know she hears you. Kiss the top of her head as she takes your coat from you.

'Give over, you daft thing!'

Don't listen. Whirl her round the room like you did on your wedding day – well, a bit slower – till you're both dizzy and laughing. It doesn't take long. Let her go and drop back into the familiar dips and depressions of your chair.

Look up as she smiles at you, breathing fast.

Reach for a cigarette.

'Be a love and put the kettle on.'

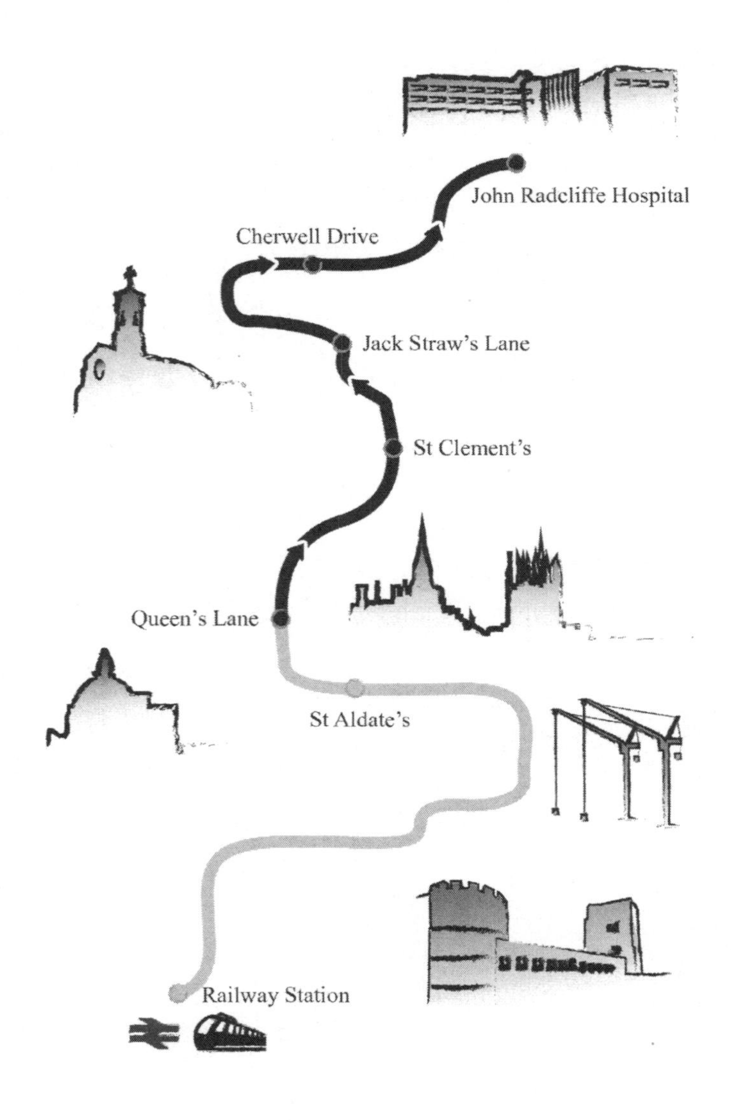
John Radcliffe Hospital
Cherwell Drive
Jack Straw's Lane
St Clement's
Queen's Lane
St Aldate's
Railway Station

No 13 Dreamcatcher

CHARLOTTE RITCHIE

She was there. John Edwards, 77, gripped the shiny aluminium bar closely as he searched for a seat. He wanted to keep his eyes on her, but the force majeure of declining years meant that he intuitively knew better than to sacrifice his love on the altar of the coveted seat. He found himself, instead, sitting next to Betty Parks, who shifted her ample body a quarter of an inch, as if to imply that it was he, not her, who was overweight.

'How are yer John?' she asked, never taking her eyes off the road ahead.

'I'm all right,' he said, glancing sideways in the hope of seeing Brenda.

Betty exhaled; a long slow shudder of breath smelling lightly of boiled eggs.

'Well, we're none of us any younger, are we?' she said.

This observation, whilst correct, was not entirely what John had wanted to hear when he'd got up that morning.

That morning, as he sat on his bed cleaning his tooth (the others were in the glass), he had daydreamed. He had daydreamed about Brenda Baker. Of course that wasn't her name now. No, now she was Brenda Washford, a widow. To the outside observer, the bus driver on the No 13, she was a slight old lady, with short silver hair, and an easy smile. No trouble at all. To John Edwards, she was Brenda Baker, the girl he'd sat next to in Mrs Williams' class. The girl whose father was the local coal merchant. The girl he had always loved. Of course they were children then, and the war had just ended. He never told her then that he loved her. He didn't know he loved her; he just always knew he wanted to be alongside her. At eleven, they'd gone their separate ways: he to East Oxford Secondary Modern, and she – for yes, she was bright as a button – to Milham Ford Grammar School for Girls. He hadn't expected to pass the eleven plus exam, and he knew he would be a tradesman like his father, but when Brenda's name was read out in assembly as one of the very few who would be going to grammar school next year, he felt his heart thud. She would not be with him at the mixed secondary modern school, she would be with the better off children; different, other, at the grammar school. He might not see her again.

The years passed. Occasionally he glimpsed her walking along with her friends, or riding a bicycle along the Marston road, but she barely seemed to recognise him, and he – how silly it seems now – was too shy to wave or call her name. Yet he had called her name. It was 1955, and the full heat of an August summer was upon them. He'd gone with his friend Alf Tanner to a party at Blossom Cottage in Old Marston. Alf knew the family, and although they were much better off than John or Alf, they had invited both of them to their son's 17th birthday party. They'd both dressed up, hoping to make an impression on the girls. John hated parties, but that evening the air was sultry, with the promise of a thunderstorm. The sitting room doors were wide open and out on the lawn, couples were dancing to a wind-up gramophone. Rock and roll, it was all the rage. Then he saw her. She was standing by herself, leaning against a cherry tree, and looking somehow awkward. He was young then. He'd been lucky with a few girls; walked out with them for a while. It had all come to nothing of course, but he had the confidence of youth then. He'd asked her to dance. It was Bill Hailey and the Comets, 'Rock around the Clock', and they were perfect together. Afterwards they sat under the tree and talked, reminisced, and eventually kissed. But then lightning, a thunderclap, people scurrying back into the house, and Brenda lost in the hurly burly.

The next time he saw her, she was walking arm in arm with Steven Washford. He cursed himself for not asking her out again that very night, or at the very least writing to her. But now it was too late. She was going out with Steven and then, she was married to him. His cousin said that Steven had got her in the family way, so they'd had to get married. He didn't care; all he knew was that she would never be his wife. Conscription came, Africa, polishing kit, spells of home leave and he'd found that he was good at something. He'd trained as an engineer. It absorbed his mind, his days and his life. It had all slipped past.

But then two weeks ago, as he stood in The High, waiting for the No 13 bus, he'd seen her. It had been raining, an April shower, and she was standing a little away from him. He watched the tilt of her head as she stretched out an arm to signal to the driver that she wanted the bus to stop. He felt his stomach tighten as she got onto the bus. He was behind her now, waiting to get on the bus. As she paid, she turned slightly. He'd smiled weakly, wondering whether she would recognise him. She'd smiled back, and said, 'Hello John. How are you?' as if sixty years had never existed.

'I'm all right,' he'd said.

'What are you up to these days?' he asked barely daring to look at her.

She smiled and said, 'I'm just on my way up to the John Radcliffe to see my new great-granddaughter.'

'Congratulations. How many great-grandchildren do you and Steven have,' he'd asked politely.

He'd never had children himself. He'd had girlfriends, lovers, hopes, but somehow he'd never found the right person.

'Well, we – well I shouldn't say 'we', because Steve died two years ago now – have got eight all together.'

John had said how sorry he was, but also how pleased he was for her, that she should have so many grandchildren.

They'd gone their separate ways. Sat in separate seats. Pretended – or at least he had – not to notice each other. He was doing the same thing now. His feelings for her were so great that he feared she would sense them, take flight, or just simply reject him. He couldn't bear failure. He'd managed these sixty years without her and he could go on doing so. She wouldn't think much of him; an old man in a tweed jacket that had passed its best. Why hadn't he seized the moment and sat down next to her? He knew the reason; it was that he was too worried about falling when the bus started, and so had sat down in the nearest seat. He could see her. She was looking at him. He smiled and half raised his hand. She patted the seat next to her. He looked at Betty Parks.

'What you waiting for John Edwards,' she said tartly.

'You and she should always have been a pair.'

He said nothing.

The bus lurched to a standstill at Jack Straw's Lane. He got up, turned around with a little difficulty, and walked towards Brenda. She was still looking at him, her eyes shining just as they had all those years ago.

'I was hoping to see you,' she said, laying her hand lightly on his knee.

oxford

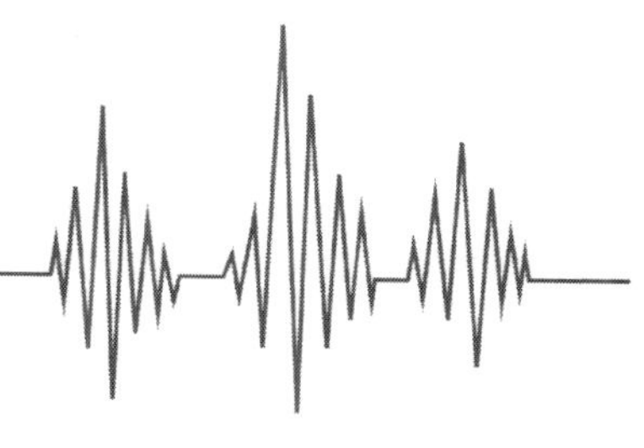

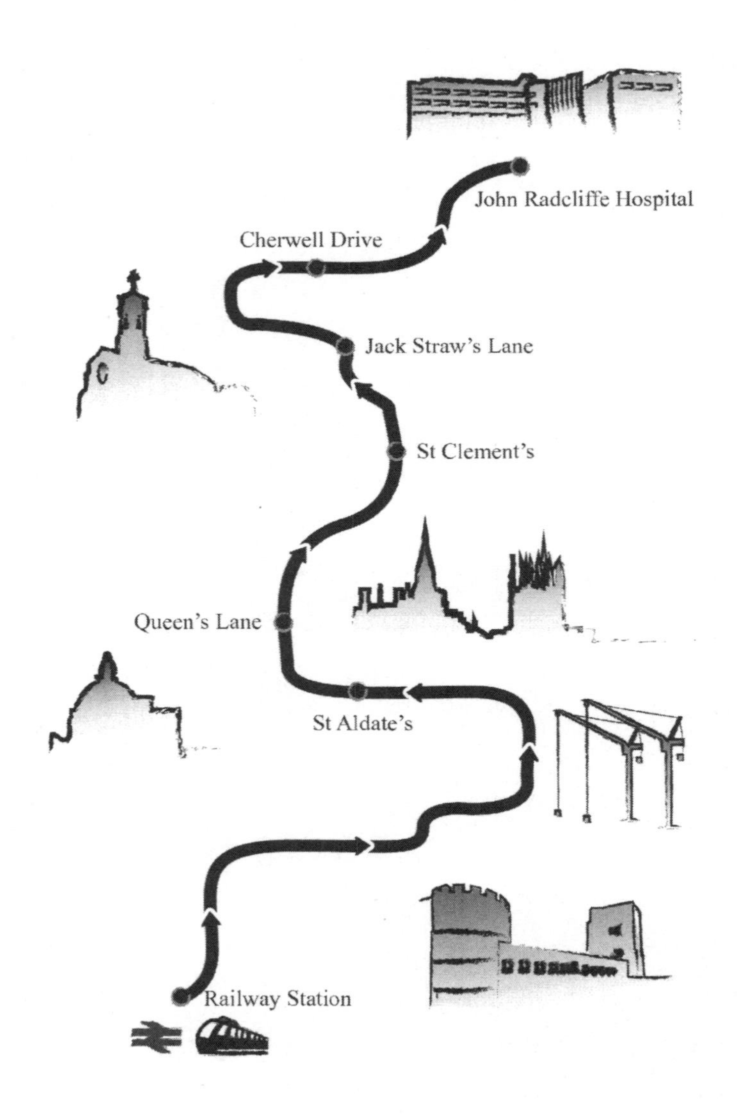
John Radcliffe Hospital
Cherwell Drive
Jack Straw's Lane
St Clement's
Queen's Lane
St Aldate's
Railway Station

Chin Up

PAULINE MASSEY

I don't mind admitting I'm scared. It's freezing standing at this bus stop. Who was it who said April is a cruel month?

March went out like a lion and it seems he's still here, roaring across the station forecourt. I have two minutes more to wait for the bus but it could be caught up in traffic. There is a part of me which hopes it is. While I'm standing at this bus stop I'm safe. I can believe that life has stood still, that I have time, that all will end well.

There are taxis queuing. It would be easy to cross the road and take one. It might get me to the hospital faster but do I want that to happen? No, I'll continue to wait for the No 13 bus, unlucky for some.

'Come in, Mister Wallace. Now let's see, when was your last consultation?'

They try to be kind. Let's face it, the staff are kind. They can see the fear on your face, perhaps they can hear the thud of your heart. You can hear it yourself in your ears, bang bang, let us live, let us live... I'm not old by today's standards, I should have more time left.

Ah, here comes the bus. It draws up beside the bus shelter and its occupants tumble off, some laughing, others pensive, some rushing for trains. The conductor nods as I place my bus pass down and wait for the green light to come on.

Then he says, 'Where's the sun then? You look frozen.'

I admit that I am and manage a smile. 'It's that sharp wind. Goes right through you. Not late today then? Traffic better while the students are away?'

All this is delaying tactics. I know what I'm up to. The longer I linger at the station, the easier it is. I am putting off having to face the truth about my condition, about what may happen in the future. Yes, I'm a coward. I'm afraid of death. I still have things I want to do. I only retired a few years ago. What if I've paid in for my pension all those years for nothing?

At the new Frideswide Square there is hooting. Now there are no controlled crossings pedestrians sometimes have to run for their lives. I see the startled expression of a young woman as she makes it to the safety of the pavement with her pushchair. I recognise that look. Perhaps I wear it all the time now. As I told you before, I am a coward. I do not want to die, not yet.

The bus is warm and my shivering has subsided. Soon we are weaving round the Westgate area. Massive cranes loom overhead; the back of the old shopping centre is devastated by the jaws of a brick-munching machine. I see an old sign advertising Shoe Zone. Things are changing in Oxford, fast. Already I find it difficult to picture the old shopping centre as it was.

At Speedwell Street I recognise an elderly man who boards the bus. He hastens to get a seat but the driver is considerate and waits for him to sit down. Perhaps he is going to the John Radcliffe too. Time is going too fast. Already we are heading up St Aldate's towards the next stop, and I notice pink blossoms coming on in Christ Church gardens.

We stop for a while and I look towards the town hall. I like this waiting. For two pins I would get off the bus and not complete the journey to the hospital. But the appointment has been made. I will see the consultant at two fifteen.

'Come in, Mister Wallace. Now let's see. When was your last consultation?'

He knows very well but it's his way of putting me at my ease. I like the doctor. What I don't like is what he has to tell me.

I look out at the bustling crowds in Cornmarket when the bus veers round into the High Street. Busy shoppers, lots of young people, tourists laughing. I envy them all. They have life ahead of them. They don't have this fear. Every morning when I wake the first thing I think of is this wretched illness. I am ashamed that I am so fearful. And I am angry too. My mind is preoccupied with this disease. It is eating away at my mind as well as my body.

Already the pink magnolia is blooming outside the university church. But it does not look good this year. Frost has browned the delicate flowers. It came out too early. Still, a tourist is taking a photo. Let the bus stop here, I think. Let us all just sit here and admire the view down the High Street.

She gets on at Queen's Lane. At first I do not recognise her. She is wearing a woollen hat which almost covers the top part of her face. She is carrying a shopping bag which has butterfly motifs all over it. And it's the bag which jogs my memory. Her name is Sally. She attends the same clinic as me.

How does she look beneath that hat? Is she pale? Have her cheeks sunk in? But when she turns and I manage to get a look I see that her face has actually filled out. Sally is looking very well. You can't go by looks, of course. And perhaps it's a blip anyway. I remember Sally telling me how frightened she was. And I pretended I wasn't. What a daft idiot.

The bus is waiting at Queen's Lane. I wonder whether there will be a change of drivers, or maybe the bus is early. I look across to the Exam Schools and wonder about the clever souls who study at Oxford. I'm a local, you see, born and bred. The area I live in was very working class once. Now it's been gentrified and the tiny two-up two-down houses are worth a fortune.

I dare not look at my watch. Time is getting on. Once the bus approaches Marston Road I know there will be little chance to enjoy the view from the window. It happens every time. My heart speeds up, I get a headache, my throat is as dry as sandpaper. Colin the coward. Colin who's frightened to go in to see the consultant in case he tells him it's curtains.

'Sorry, Mr Wallace, but I have to tell you, you only have a few months to live.'

'Hello, Colin, isn't it? I remember you from the clinic a couple of months ago.'

Sally has come to sit next to me. She recognised me.

'Yes, that's right. Just on my way to see the consultant again.'

'And you're scared, right?'

What was the point in pretending? 'Yes, I'm scared. I'll get my test results today.'

'I was trembling so much the last time I went the nurse told me to take lots of deep breaths.'

I didn't like to ask Sally how she had fared. 'Oh, right.' I hesitated. 'Are you going to the clinic today?'

'No, nothing like that. I'm working for the League of Friends now.'

'Are you?'

Sally must have noticed my surprise. 'Don't look so shocked, Colin. This could be you in a couple of months' time. Have they put you on the trial yet?'

'No, but the consultant mentioned something about it last time.'

'Do it, Colin. I'm so much better already. I've got more energy. Must have, mustn't I, if I can work in the café? Doctor told me things are looking good.'

'You certainly look much better, Sally. I'm pleased for you.'

'That's the good thing about living in Oxford. All the top brains, and the opportunity to take part in new treatments. We're the lucky ones, Colin.'

'Yes, I suppose so.'

The No 13 is now moving through Northway Estate. I hate this last bit of the journey. No way of stopping the bus now. It carries on its relentless route towards the main entrance of the John Radcliffe hospital. We are already at the West Wing. Sally is preparing to get off the bus.

She says, 'Come and see me afterwards, Colin. I'll treat you to a cuppa and a currant bun.' She pats me on the shoulder. 'Chin up, lad.'

They are magic words, and how does she know them? That's what my old dad used to say to me when I was a boy, 'Chin up, lad.' He was a lovely man. Worked on the railway most of his life, helping to repair those great steam engines.

The bus is drawing away from its penultimate stop. Now we are heading up the hill towards the main entrance. Something has changed. I am not afraid. I will go to the waiting room and sit until I am called to see the consultant. And if he offers me the chance of taking part in a trial I will say yes. I'm looking forward to seeing Sally afterwards at the café. Chin up, lad! Thirteen isn't always an unlucky number.

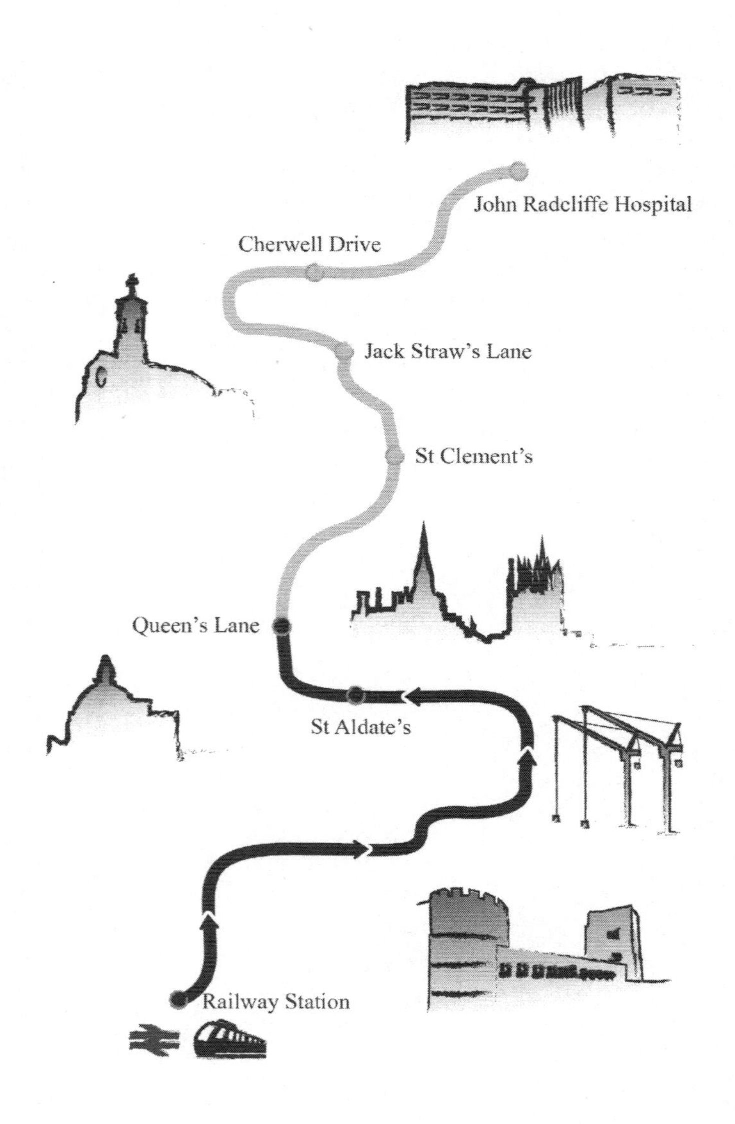
John Radcliffe Hospital
Cherwell Drive
Jack Straw's Lane
St Clement's
Queen's Lane
St Aldate's
Railway Station

The Untravelled Road

REBECCA HOTCHEN

When her teacher announced that there would be no double Chemistry next week, the idea came to Lucja in an immediate rush. She stayed at the school library that night, looking up train and bus times, making notes on how long it would take and memorizing maps with the same ferocity that had seen her pass the university's stringent admission test only a few short months ago. She didn't want to use the computer at home, in case her Mum looked over her shoulder and saw what she was doing. She'd never been that far on her own before, and she was certain her Mum wouldn't allow it. Even Ina had never been so far, and she was two years older than Lucja.

Emily was willing to come with her, although her classes hadn't been cancelled. There was no surprise here: normally, it would be Emily suggesting something mad and Lucja reluctantly agreeing. In the morning, they both slung their school bags over their shoulders and headed out to sixth form as nonchalantly as possible, feeling that every creak in their voice would give them away. They didn't dare voice their rebellion aloud, so when they met up they both just nodded, and turned down the path away from the school and towards the train station in silence. At every footstep echoing behind them, their gazes darted back. Each time confirmed what they knew: no one was following. Of course no one was following.

As they reached the small station, both girls had to suppress giggles at their success. Lucja was swept up in her new-found streak of recklessness, but she came back to earth with a resounding crash when they heard the price of the tickets.

'Each?' she asked, in shock. 'Seventy pounds *each*?'

The man behind the counter did not appear to sympathize with their shock. 'Oxford's hardly the next town over,' he said. 'If you've got a railcard, it'll only be around fifty pounds.' He looked at them expectantly, before adding with a warning tone, 'Each.'

A queue was forming behind them, so they shuffled to one side and dug through their purses. 'I feel so stupid,' Lucja lamented. 'I should have thought to check the prices properly. I must have been looking at one-way tickets or something.' She continued to berate herself in a quiet hiss while they counted their money. 'I could go into my savings, but I feel like I'm going to need every penny of that…' Lucja said reluctantly, already starting to talk herself out of the whole thing. What would be the point of going up now? It would make no difference, and if she didn't get the grades in August, then it would have been a complete waste.

'How much do you have?' Emily asked.

Lucja stared at what was in her hands. 'Thirty-seven fifty. Not even close to being able to buy one ticket, never mind having to pay for buses and things once I get there.'

Emily tipped her purse over Lucja's open hands. 'Well, now you've got at least sixty quid. It's not going to be luxury or anything, but you shouldn't need much if you're only up for a day.'

'I can't—'

'Yes you can,' Emily interrupted forcefully. 'You wouldn't have suggested going if it wasn't important to you, Lucja. We've been best friends since you still had an accent, and I'm going to miss the hell out of you when you're in Oxford swotting up. The only thing that will make it bearable is if I know you're happy up there.'

There were a lot of coins, and the man behind the counter slid each one over slowly and suspiciously, but eventually he had counted out enough and he printed a return ticket. 'Train leaves in twenty minutes from platform two,' he said primly.

Lucja and Emily milled over to the platform. 'Thanks, Em,' Lucja said quietly. 'I really could have got the money out from the bank, if I had to.'

'Think of it as an early birthday present,' Emily said with a small smile. 'Definitely better than the tat I normally end up buying you, right? Half a ticket to Oxford, now that's generosity.'

The train pulled up and Lucja boarded. Out of the train window, she could see Emily chasing the train, waving a piece of paper in lieu of a handkerchief, and making a big production out of blowing kisses and wiping away non-existent tears. Laughing, Lucja folded herself into a seat at a table and waved back. The early morning commuters that were dotted around the carriage turned to glare at Lucja, so she slid a hand over her mouth to stifle her laughter.

Thinking about the length of the train ride, and how late she could get away with getting back, Lucja knew she wouldn't have very long in Oxford at all. She wondered if it would be worth the money and the hassle just to have spent a few hours there, but she knew it would. When she'd been a little girl, first moving to England, everything had been new and alien to her, not least the language. It had taken years for her tiny town to feel anything like home, and leaving it behind for land unchartered was terrifying. There would be no mum, no big sister, no little brother, to be her anchor this time. At least today she could see more than the inside of one college, and the town tarted up with its best face on and full of prospective students on open day. Today would be a normal day for Oxford, and she'd finally have a chance to see it as a place to call home instead of a momentous symbol of her future.

The schoolbooks that Lucja had brought along as props were soon spread out on the table. Studying was a distraction while she sped closer and closer towards that future. She didn't really notice how hungry she was growing until the food cart rattled past. Her stomach growled, but she ignored it, very aware of the little change left over from the price of the ticket. She forcibly turned her attention back to her notes but could no longer concentrate. She mouthed the words, compelling her mind to take it in, but was grateful when her phone announced a text message.

'U there yet? Xx,' it was from Emily.

'Almost! It's so boring without you. Xx.'

Lucja assumed that Emily hadn't gone back to class when it turned out she couldn't go up to Oxford. Either that, or she was in class and paying very little attention, based on the speed with which she was muscles. People in yellow jackets belied the disaster, gesturing mysteriously to cranes and leading them through the wreckage.

There was a long wait to filter through, but at last they were moving again in two-way traffic. Oxford seemed so ordinary, Lucja thought, taking in the large characterless buildings nearby. Nothing here would make her think she was somewhere new. Until the bus turned.

Up ahead, there was a huge domed building. A break in the clouds lit it from behind, painting a stark silhouette against the sky. It was stunning, exactly as majestic as Lucja remembered Oxford to be and more. Before it lay green fields, filled with people laughing and talking in groups, taking photographs and pointing. Lucja drew her phone out and took a quick picture herself. She sent it to Emily, with the caption, 'Definitely in Oxford now! Xx.' She placed the phone on the seat behind her, anticipating a quick reply.

They inched up the road, giving Lucja as much time as she needed to get her fill of the magnificent architecture. Anther grand building stood ahead of her, its flag white with a simple outline of an ox blowing furiously in the wind. It did not hold her attention in the same way, and Lucja kept her eyes on the dome, drinking it in.

Lucja's hand reached automatically for her phone and came up empty. She turned to look. There was nothing there. Her stomach dropped and she leapt to her feet and looked under her seat. Nothing. She checked her bag, kneeling in the aisle and piling her books beside her. It wasn't there. Her heart was in her throat. She looked around. The bus was about half full. There was no way to tell who the person who'd taken her phone was.

This trip, which had always felt like a risk, suddenly seemed like the stupid whim of a stupid child. She blinked away tears, slowly sorting her books back into her bag and trying to keep her breath even. On top of the money – almost as much she made in a week as a waitress – now it had cost the phone that her mum had bought her as a combined present for Christmas and passing her admission test. She didn't deserve to get into Oxford, Lucja thought, if she made such terrible choices.

She felt alone, adrift, as though a lifeline had been cut. Oxford suddenly seemed much further away from home now that she had no way to contact Emily, or even her Mum, if things started to go wrong. She tried to quell her panic enough to remember her Mum's mobile number, but she couldn't. Lucja felt real fear rising within her at the magnitude of being in a strange town without her main means of contact.

Her bus continued its steady progress through heavy traffic.

She had left the typical and familiar behind entirely. Her eyes took in pretty painted buildings, huge imposing colleges with twisted dry-mouthed gargoyles, spires, and domes. This was the Oxford she remembered, the Oxford that awed and intimidated her, making her feel tiny, a mere speck in time compared to the centuries that these stones had seen. Seeing it now was like taking a bite of cake to find it was nothing but ash. The excitement she had felt at the sight of the first domed building was completely lost. She wondered if she ought to just give up now and head back. What could be gained from staying?

And then she heard it. The familiar chirp of her phone's text alert. It came from in front of her; a young couple sat immediately before her, and a mother and child right at the front. Neither the couple nor the mother looked guilty. The child on the other hand...

He was gazing down at his lap intently. Lucja stood and peered around. It was there! Her heart started thudding in her chest.

'Excuse me,' she said, as politely as she could manage, her panic not quite evaporated and her voice unusually tight. 'I think your son has picked up my phone by mistake.'

A few other passengers craned their necks to watch with some interest, and the young mother's face grew red.

firing texts back. It was a relief for Lucja to have the familiar humour of her friend with her.

The next stop was Oxford. Lucja got to her feet and waited at the door, aware that she could be standing for a long time, but too nervous she would miss it to wait in her seat. Others crowded round her, and Lucja could feel the tension in them to disembark.

The doors slid open with a hiss. A rush of people pushed past Lucja, and she hurried to join them on the platform. Disoriented, it took her some time to see the way out. She fed her ticket to the barriers, and finally could see through the doors to Oxford beyond. She was here.

Her heart thumped with each step. There was a list of potential buses in her bag, but she didn't reach for it. She had them memorized. As she descended the steps, a pillar-box red double-decker swung around the corner and stopped a little ahead of her. In warm orange lights, the number thirteen was clearly visible. Lucja quickened her steps, but needn't have done so. The engine switched off, and the driver sidled out and vanished before she could board. She waited anxiously, checking her watch constantly, eager to be on her way. She wondered if she'd be better off walking. It would certainly be quicker; her only concern was getting lost.

Lucja had just made up her mind to try to walk – already rooting around in her bag for her map – when the driver came back. There were several people boarding ahead of

Lucja, and she made certain to listen carefully both to what they said, and to the prices.

'Single to the city centre, please,' Lucja said, counting out the fare precisely. She climbed the stairs to the upper deck, to have a better view of the city. She sat just in front of the staircase, with a bell nearby so that she would be able to get off quickly. An examination of her ticket told her that her stop would be called Queen's Lane.

The bus pulled away from the station, looping round to the main road. The last few times she had been to Oxford, Lucja had paid little attention to the bus's route, her nose stuck in notes while she let her Mum do all the navigating. Now, Lucja examined everything around her, hoping to gain some insight into the city. There was a large glass-fronted building on her left, but they moved past it too quickly for her to see what it was. Up ahead, she saw a Korean restaurant on the corner; Lucja had never had Korean food before. There was not a great variation in food types where she'd grown up. She wondered if Oxford might also have a Polish restaurant.

The streets they sailed through now were less majestic than Lucja had expected. She supposed that Oxford couldn't be all cobblestones and gargoyles, that it must have normal shops and houses too. The bus came to a stop, and from her vantage point, it was possible to make out an odd green mound. A poster fitted to the fence surrounding the steep hill invited her to unlock Oxford's history by taking a tour of the castle. Excitedly, Lucja gazed out the window, and as they pulled away, she saw the castle's high grey walls. She doubted she'd be able to afford to visit it today, but she made a mental note to do so when – if – she moved.

There was an abrupt stop and a loud horn. Given the crowded pedestrian walkway ahead, Lucja assumed people must be crossing the road in front of them. Here, there was a maze of construction work. The torn up building looked like something from a disaster film, beams sticking out from concrete like exposed bones broken clean of flesh and

'I don't know what you mean,' she said, not looking at her son. 'Accusing my boy of something like that, you should be ashamed.'

At a loss for what to say, Lucja looked at the child. He was hastily trying to squirrel the phone away into his jacket. *No you don't*, she thought.

'I mean,' Lucja said crisply and loudly, 'the phone I can see in his hands right now. Perhaps he picked it up by mistake, but you are doing him no favours teaching him he doesn't need to give it back.'

She held her breath, waiting to see what the mother would say next.

She said nothing. Instead, the boy himself volunteered the phone, while his mother watched on with a sour expression. Lucja was about to say something more when the bell dinged. She swept down the stairs, glad for the opportunity to leave. Passengers were filing off, and Lucja joined them. She was light, free, and the city—though strange—seemed now to call to her, to spread its arms wide in welcome. There was no cloak of anxiety heavy over Lucja's shoulders now, with her phone clutched safely in one hand, adrenalin from her confrontation still running through her. She thanked the driver off-handedly and her foot hit the pavement one year later.

'Mum, Leo, this way,' Lucja called over her shoulder, turning right so they could stop at one of the cafés nearby. Ina was walking beside her. Casually, comfortably, and with the confidence of a resident, Lucja led the way up the path with her family around her. After a year here, there was little hesitancy left in her movements.

'Stop, let us catch up!' her Mum said, laughing. Her voice had never lost its accent, and it warmed Lucja now to hear it in person, after a whole semester of it being muffled by distance.

Lucja slowed, and her Mum stepped up beside her. She placed her hands on Lucja's shoulders and gazed at her seriously, face bright with pride. 'You have come very far,' she said in a voice thick with emotion.

'It is far,' she said quietly, her mind on that day around a year ago when she had travelled down alone, half-funded by Emily, 'but it's okay. I know my way now.'

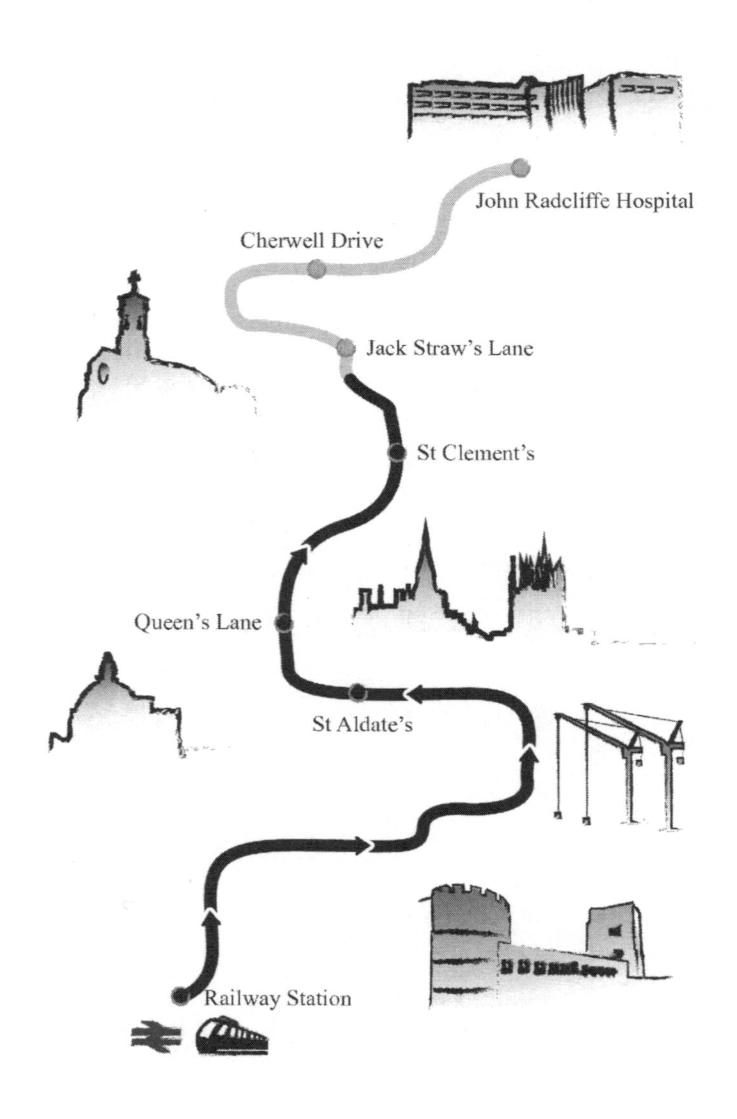
John Radcliffe Hospital
Cherwell Drive
Jack Straw's Lane
St Clement's
Queen's Lane
St Aldate's
Railway Station

The Petrov Defence

MARIA MATE

'Are you ready for the battle tonight?' I asked Csabi when we were settled on the back seat of the bus. He was coming to stay with me for a few days and I had just met him at the station.

'Sure I am,' he said. 'Beating Didcot last week has got me really fired up! But tell me. How was your visit home? Did you manage to sell your house in Szentendre?'

'Yes, I did! It was about time, too. But I will miss swimming in the Danube.' I am a very keen swimmer and still couldn't believe what I had done.

'There are plenty of swimming pools in England but it's not the same, I know. Back home there are natural hot springs everywhere - so invigorating.'

'Very true,' I said. 'But nothing beats the Danube... Pst, look!' I suddenly touched his arm and whispered 'Look what those two are up to.' Csabi dragged his attention from the cranes towering over the new Westgate development and looked at the two men facing us. They had their eyes closed and were smiling faintly to themselves. They seemed to be talking in code.

'Knight f3,' one of them said quietly, but loud enough for us to hear.

'Knight f6,' the other one replied immediately.

'Knight takes pawn.'

There was a pause while the bus stopped in St Aldate's for more passengers. An elderly lady struggled towards the back and sat across the aisle from me and Csabi. I could see her eying the two men suspiciously.

'Bishop g4.'

She looked at the speaker intently then glanced around to see what could have provoked such an extraordinary remark. But it was just another busy day in High Street with delivery vehicles, taxis and other buses slowing progress. As they gathered speed outside the Mitre his companion suddenly said:

'Rook e1!'

Seeing that both men had their eyes closed, she stared at them unashamedly.

'Then f5.' This was as they passed the Old Bank Hotel.

Both men opened their eyes briefly when the bus stopped at Queen's Lane and, in the silence, their peculiar conversation attracted the attention of one or two other passengers. I found this very amusing because I knew exactly what was happening.

Outside Magdalen College there was a rush of coded remarks which made both men smile to themselves. I smiled too but it clearly worried the elderly lady. Discreetly, she took a notebook from her handbag and began writing in it.

'Don't you know what they are doing? Listen, Csabi!' I said. He concentrated hard.

'Knight takes pawn.'

'Bishop takes pawn on h2 check!'

'Okey dokey artichokey, king recaptures!'

'Vow!' said Csabi, 'I couldn't understand what they were saying but it all makes sense now' and a grin spread from ear to ear.

'One more reason to improve your English!' I couldn't suppress the teacher in me. I think it is simply unacceptable that people come to live here but still don't learn the language properly. I've been nagging Csabi for years but he doesn't seem to get any better.

'I know those guys,' I whispered to him. 'They are members of Oxford City but they sometimes come to the Cowley club. They might be there tonight.'

'Good! What are they like?' Csabi asked.

'The tall one never remembers anything. He's a nice chap but a bit absent-minded. People joke that he can't even remember his own name, but when he's playing he can be a real demon.'

'What about the other one? Is he any good?'

'Yes, he is. But he talks too much, telling jokes all the time. Probably to put off his opponents.'

'I hope I'll get a chance to play him.'

'The team says he's a bit of a weirdo,' I went on, moving closer to Csabi. 'They claim he can move his ears if he wants to.'

'Golly!' Csabi sounded almost envious. 'Why are you still whispering? They don't understand Hungarian, surely?'

'No, but I don't want to distract them. I want to listen to the game.'

There was another quick-fire exchange as we passed the new Centre for Islamic Studies in Marston Road. Wide-eyed now, the lady scribbled furiously in her notebook. I would have loved to know what she was writing, but we had to get off at the Somerset.

For us, though, that wasn't the end of the story because, as Csabi and I took the bus back into Oxford later that day, we were surprised to see the same two men were on it as well. And they were still playing the game, talking in code. Like us, they got off at Queen's Lane, crossed the road, and waited for the Rose Hill bus. So they were coming to the club, too.

When the bus arrived, we sat behind them, so we could follow their game. They were so absorbed in what they were doing that they were completely oblivious to their surroundings. In their mind they had to maintain a picture of the pieces left on the board and all the recent moves; it takes a lot of concentration.

There wasn't much action until we rounded the Plain, then the tall one loudly challenged 'Knight takes bishop on d3.' But it earned him a quick riposte. Things were getting exciting now.

'I think they've been playing all day,' I said. 'They must be exhausted.'

'Yes. The old Petrov can go on forever.'

'Queen takes bishop. Easy-peasy, lemon-squeezy!' the tall one called out triumphantly. But he spoke too soon.

'Queen h4 check!' The game was over and the tall one resigned.

'Fantastic!' I exclaimed. The contestants turned to me in amazement and we all started laughing. 'Sorry,' I said, 'I was following your game – it was so exciting!'

'Are you coming to the club, too?' asked the short one. 'I thought I had seen you before.' I explained that in Hungary it was almost our national game, and that I had been a member of the Cowley club for several years. We got off the bus and walked together the short distance to Rose Hill Methodist Church.

'I am surprised they let us play in a church,' said Csabi. 'It is such an aggressive game.'

'Perhaps they don't know what we get up to,' I giggled.

'Especially with players as aggressive as these two,' Csabi added, and everyone laughed again.

'And talking of aggression,' I said to Csabi, 'I am expecting someone here I would like you to meet.'

'Let me guess. You mean… Magnus Carlsen?' he asked.

'Well, I'm not sure the world champion will be here, but you never know...'

'Then you'll have to put up with me, I'm afraid!' It was Joseph, my former Hungarian coach, who was also visiting Oxford. He may not be the world champion but he was certainly a leading player. I introduced him to Csabi and they shook hands in the special way Hungarian men always do, then sat down at one of the many boards ready for the tournament.

'Shall we have a quick warm-up before we start?' Csabi challenged Joseph.

'Sure, but we don't really need a board, do we?'

'Right, we'll play blindfold.' Csabi was eager to test Joseph's playing strength. 'But we'll have to make it a quick one, not like those two on the bus.'

'OK. Five minutes. What's your favourite opening?'

'The Petrov – with my secret variation!' They turned round with their backs to each other.

'Can I watch the game?' I asked.

'Only if you keep your eyes closed,' said Joseph.

He stared at the ceiling, Csabi at the floor, each determined to defeat the other. Their moves came thick and fast, like an artillery exchange. They were going to exploit any weakness and use every opportunity to crush their opponent.

That's the way it is with chess.

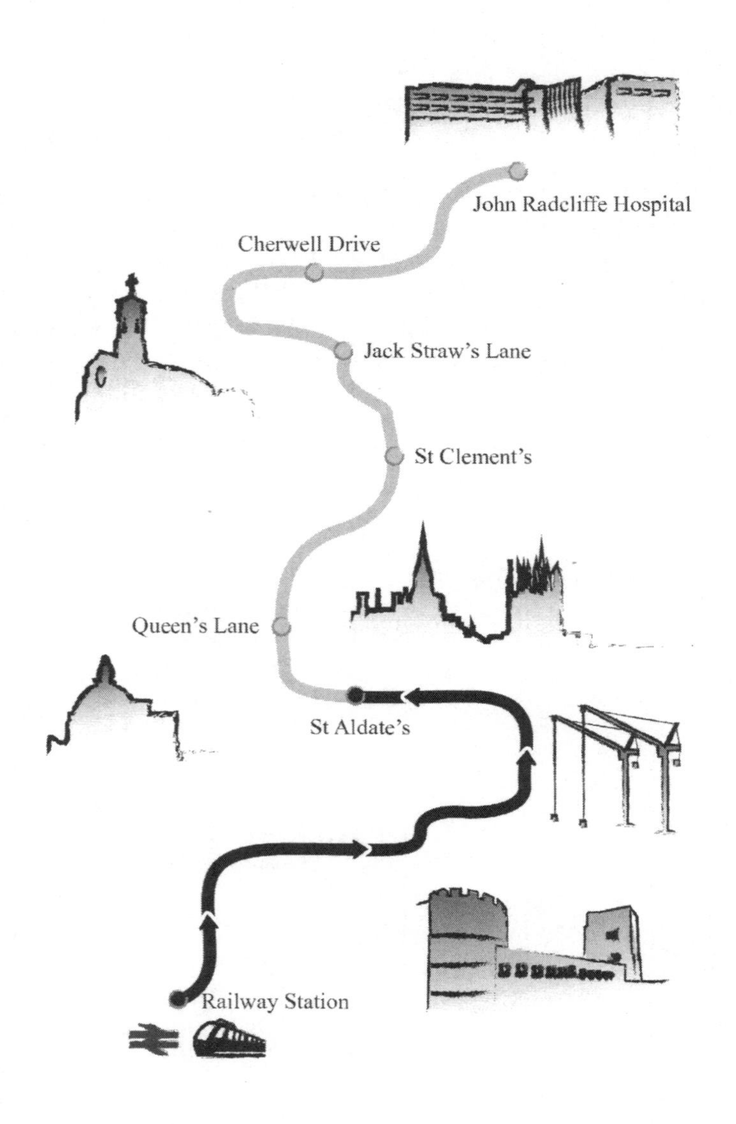
John Radcliffe Hospital
Cherwell Drive
Jack Straw's Lane
St Clement's
Queen's Lane
St Aldate's
Railway Station

After the Experiment

JESSICA WOODWARD

'Excuse me, miss?'

My head shot up and I squeaked, 'Whatever it is, no!' before realising that the person speaking was not a leafleter or a promoter or a data-collector, but a station employee giving back a coin that had fallen from my pocket. Flushed with embarrassment, I thanked him and scurried out into the car park, not daring to look back in case the incredulous male chuckles I thought I could hear were his. I felt deep shame that the nerves were already stirring, when I had barely reached Oxford, but I could never manage to hear that common phrase without remembering.

Hovering behind a pillar, I found an Oxfordshire bus timetable on my phone and examined the available options for travelling to my friend's dance event in St Clement's. Several buses were parked close by. For a moment, the choice seemed momentous. Crashes, rampaging criminal passengers, freak storms and lightning strikes, familiar faces... the most hideous possibilities flicked through my mind.

I remembered that Oswald used to claim 13 as his lucky number because no one else cared for it. Perhaps in this instance, I would follow my distant husband's judgement, because in Oxford I could not trust my own.

The Royal Oxford Hotel

I staggered up the stairs of the No 13 bus and sank into the nearest pair of seats, squeezing in among my bags of the sparkly belts and wristbands that my dance pupils loved to borrow for Zumba songs. My eye caught the headline of a magazine that lay crumpled on the floor and a pang of horror shot through me.

'PHILIP AT 95' – not surprising and not intended to be distressing. Most people would know that Prince Philip's birthday was approaching and most people would be delighted for him. But for me, any mention of that regal trigger who (albeit unknowingly) had catapulted me into the depths of ridicule led to a thumping heart and creeping dread.

I looked around. Passengers were chatting, texting and pondering. I recognised none of them, and none seemed to be paying attention to me or the magazine. I ought to have remained calm, I ought to have laughed at myself for imagining omens twice in the space of five minutes, but something did not feel safe.

The bus was trundling towards a large building emblazoned with silver letters. Grotesquely, I realised that one of the words read 'ROYAL'.

Twenty Years Earlier

'Excuse me, miss?'

The anthropologist's young wife paused in the station doorway with a shy smile. Two women in navy-blue Oxford University T-shirts were seeking her attention. One held out a leaflet.

'You look like a first-year student,' grinned the leaflet-holder. 'Am I right?'

'No, I'm just popping over to Oxford to clear out my husband's office.'

'Your husband?' The mutual eyebrow-raise between the two promoters was meant to be subtle, but the anthropologist's wife knew that some people were startled by marriage at her age and was inured to such signs.

'He's an anthropological researcher. He's just left for Nevada to look for evidence for his next book.'

'And are you at the university?'

'No, I've never studied for a degree.'

'And do you work at all?' The leaflet-holder's mouth was twisting with something like amusement and the anthropologist's wife felt an old lurking worry about appearing naïve.

'I work for a local dance studio. I help to run the classes. The children's classes and the adult ones.'

'Ah. Well, anyway, with your university connection, perhaps you would be interested in participating in our experiment.' The wife felt the leaflet thrust into her hand. On the front of it was a word she recognised from various documents Oswald had left at home. She had been wondering what it meant, but was not going to admit her ignorance to these two.

'That looks very interesting.'

'It does, doesn't it? Do read through the leaflet when you get home and call us if you'd like to sign up.'

'Thank you.'

The idea of contributing to university research nagged at the anthropologist's wife's mind throughout the forty-five-minute walk to Oswald's department. Her sixth-form days replayed themselves to her; the toil that had gone into all those English essays, only for the result paper to come through with a cold, hard 'D'.

'You're far too simple and straightforward, Tasha,' her teacher had sighed. Well, what if fate was giving her a chance to do away with that image? She could have Oxford University on her CV instead of just being married to someone who worked there. Perhaps it might even compensate for her dream of applying for an English degree, which had withered away.

By the time she reached Oswald's office, she had stolen enough glances at the leaflet while waiting to cross roads to know that the experiment involved writing, and that no advanced qualifications were necessary. Her heart was fluttering. Ambition that had been dulled for two years by her romance with Oswald was once again coursing through her. She picked up Oswald's telephone and dialled the number on the leaflet, picturing that teacher's surprise when her name appeared in newspapers as a contributor to a scientific breakthrough at Oxford.

Oxford Castle

Not long after the Royal Oxford Hotel, the bus paused outside a castle, allowing itself to be overtaken by the No 5, which seemed to be following an identical route. Apparently, a different choice of bus would have been no more peaceful; a non-driver could not economically reach the East Oxford Zumba Party without passing symbols of monarchy.

Another shock hit me when I noticed that attached to the front wall of the castle was a sign proclaiming 'Oxford Central Library has moved to the Castle Quarter.' A library. It was as if the one thing that could have saved me in pre-Internet Oxford was being waved in front of me as a taunt.

Twenty Years Earlier

'Before we proceed any further, we need you to reconfirm that you understand the nature of this study and that you are happy to take part in it.' The leaflet-holder was reading from a sheet of paper which had an 'Oxford University Ethics Committee' stamp and several unreadable signatures at the bottom. It had turned out that she was the leader of the project.

'Oh yes, I'm very happy to take part.'

'Wonderful. So here are the materials you can use to inspire your essay.' She placed a pile of sombre hardbacks on the seminar-room table. 'And remember, this is a study on...' she used that word from Oswald's papers that Tasha had kept meaning to look up, 'so try to take as much inspiration from them as you can. You have three hours.'

As the door clicked shut behind the student, Tasha examined the titles of the books. They all seemed to be about cargo cults, whatever those were. John Frum, Tom Navy, Turaga.... names she didn't recognise. Bateri, Prince Philip... Prince Philip! Even she knew who he was. She chose that book and skimmed through the pages, acquiring chunks of inspiration just as the student had told her to do. She learnt of faraway tribes who worshipped things that other people found ordinary. To his compatriots, Prince Philip was a man, but to a village on the other side of the globe, he was a divine being who created all.

After half an hour, she was ready to write. The experience was thrilling. If only that stupid teacher had known the proper university techniques, her English A Level would never have been so humiliating. This was blissfully simple; choosing the words was effortless; she had found the method that worked for her. In fact, she felt a glimmer of temptation to submit the application that only two years before had seemed hopeless.

Queen Street

After the castle, the bus veered past a buzzing shopping area and into a gap between a modern office block and a building site. The street sign for the shopping area made me wince: Queen Street. *The Prince Philip Movement of Vanuatu believe that their god, Philip, has fulfilled the prophecy of marrying a powerful queen...* My brain screamed at itself to stop, but memories were pushing themselves at me from every direction.

I spotted a newspaper stand tucked away on a quieter corner. The headline had been the first clue to the seriousness of my mistake. It was on only one paper, but that paper was a notorious one that fed off even the obscurest mistakes made in Oxford. They had positioned the headline in a black box to the right of the political news, with what appeared to be Oswald's passport photo above.

After I changed my Christian name and reverted to my maiden surname, and undertook sessions with a psychiatrist, I had felt almost cured of the shame. The headline and the A Level result and Oswald's long-distance application for a divorce because I had made such a fool out of him; those things had filled my mind less and less. I had thought I had the confidence to come to Oxford and assist my friend in the running of her Zumba Party. And now one single bus journey was shattering the wall I had built up between my new self and Tasha, forcing me to live out the failure again.

Oxford University anthropologist's wife plagiarises world-famous book on Philip worshippers. I could see it as if today's newspapers still said it. Plagiarism: that was the word I could have looked up, but hadn't.

Twenty Years Earlier

A scholarly head peered around the gnarled medieval door. 'Good afternoon. You must be Tasha. Come in and sit on the sofa.'

Tasha tiptoed in, her mind a tumult of awe and nervousness. One academic was already settled in a decaying green armchair; the other, who had welcomed her, angled himself on a purple chaise longue and flicked his hand as if to hurry her to sit down. She sat and felt herself sinking; the sofa was extremely soft. She had not expected such comfort at one of these admissions interviews. Oswald had always told her they were intended to be gruelling; how surprised he would be when they next spoke, to discover that she had attempted one.

The two academics introduced themselves, then fixed each other in a cryptic gaze. Eventually, the chaise longue one spoke again in quiet, ponderous tones.

'I wonder if you can guess why we wanted to meet with you today, Tasha.'

'I'd like to apply for the English course.'

'Yes, we know that. But it was your sample essay we particularly wished to discuss. We thought it was very good, and it didn't seem to reflect your A Level grade.'

'Do you mean my Prince Philip essay?'

'Yes.' He let a long pause fall before continuing. 'Can you tell me how you went about writing it?'

Tasha felt an impromptu surge of confidence and determination. This was her sole chance to be all that she wanted to be. She was not going to let it escape her through false modesty.

'I actually wrote it as part of an Oxford University research study,' she announced proudly. 'I don't know if you heard about it – the plagiarism study? They explored how people write essays using the plagiarism technique, then showed them to different readers, in order to see how easy it is to tell when the technique has been used.'

'Ah.' The chaise longue scholar looked rueful.

Snorts and splutters erupted from the green armchair. The other academic could contain her derision no longer.

Turn Again Lane

If I had previously had no suspicion of what I had done, the ensuing explanation made it painfully obvious. It was so logical and yet so easy to overlook. The worst aspect was that the fault was all my own; no one could argue that the leaflet had not said what the experiment was about. Self-fulfilling prophecy was something I now well understood. I had been so cowed by my fear of appearing ignorant that I had subconsciously ignored every opportunity for it not to happen.

The bus was still forging ahead and another road sign rose into view. Turn Again Lane. I wondered how long it would take me to turn again into the ordinary woman I had constructed before today.

We jolted around a corner. A wave of nausea flooded through me. I felt a sudden wish to breathe clean, natural air. The passenger in front of me – a dark-haired woman in a red cardigan – was saying something about meadows into her mobile phone.

'No, Mother, it's no use getting off at Christ Church Meadows. I said that's the next stop, not Hector's stop. He'll get off at his old college like he always does. Honestly, Mother, I despair of him.'

I jammed the red 'STOP' button, gathered my bags and steeled my stomach for the stairs. As the bus halted and I began to totter down, I heard the woman wail, 'Oh, Mother, I just want a normal husband!'

I would have liked to have a husband at all. After I had informed him that my belongings were cleared out of our home, Oswald had made himself un-contactable. Last time I looked at his web page, I hadn't even been able to tell if he still worked in Oxford.

Christ Church Meadows

I stumbled through green, gulping down the revival that the light and the breeze brought. When my brain cleared enough to think seriously of the time, I checked my watch and realised that the bus ride had been shorter than I had imagined; I had still had forty minutes left to reach St Clement's. With relief, I flopped onto a bench. Sounds started to filter back into my ears. Feet shuffling on gravel, exclamations, guffaws. One word crowed louder than the others: 'Reunion!'

I turned. An elderly crowd in lounge suits and floral dresses was edging down a path that led to a black wrought-iron gate. They were all beaming in that glazed way that suggests an effort to be exceptionally social. Again I wished I could be the type of person who laughed at unnerving tricks of the mind. So many things that were harmless at heart carried fearful associations for me: ancient former students retreading college grounds after decades, glossy magazines designed to warm hearts with palaces and romance, station workers trying to demonstrate good customer care. I needed to draw an un-crossable line against the past.

My sickness was turning into tiredness; my eyelids were drooping. Reunion... Oswald... the leaflet-holder... the school teacher... the chaise longue... the green armchair... Prince Philip... Oswald...

My eyes snapped open again. The crowd had trickled through the gate and alone on the gravel path was a familiar figure, staring at me in amazement and recognition.

'Tasha?'

There was a reunion in store for me too, and suddenly I realised that one way to conquer the past was to try and obliterate it with newer, happier memories. He looked as if he was having the same thought.

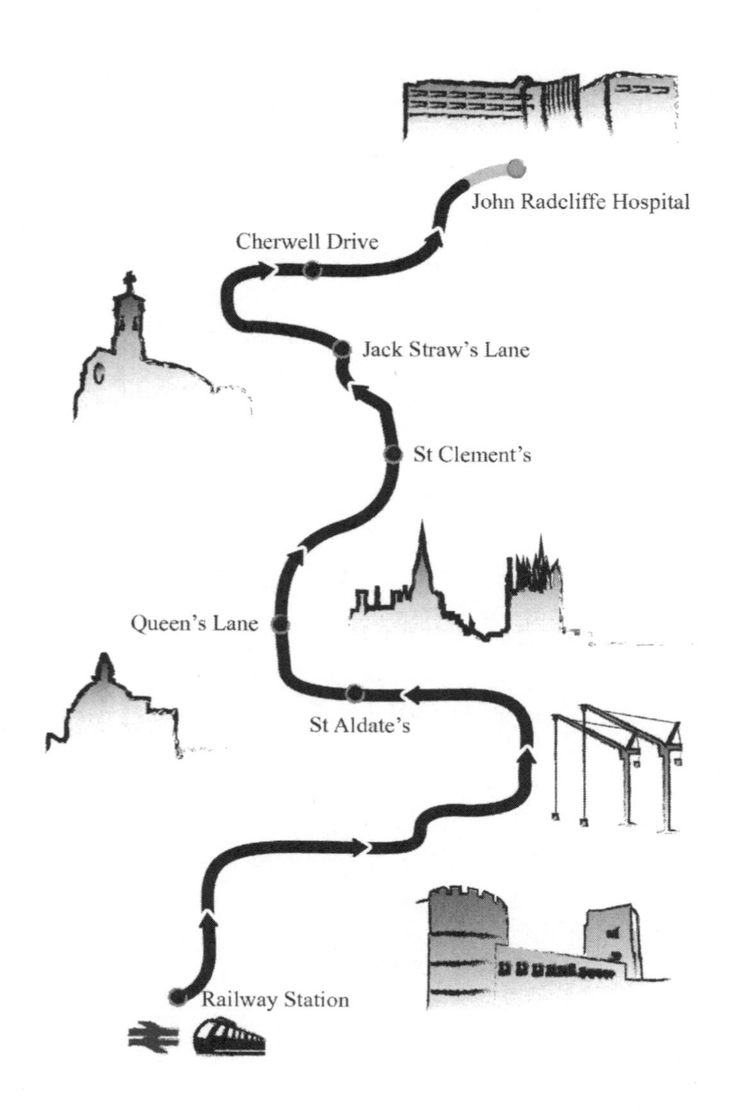
John Radcliffe Hospital
Cherwell Drive
Jack Straw's Lane
St Clement's
Queen's Lane
St Aldate's
Railway Station

Cold Fresh Drinking Water

KAREN GRAY

Eventually, Jenny was back on the bus, settled into her usual seat with her case by her side, forehead pressed against the smooth glass of the window. The No 13 hummed off on its routine trawl backwards and forwards between the station and the JR, gathering up passengers at one stop, relinquishing them at another.

I'm a creature of habit, she thought as she watched the familiar street scenes shifting past. *Just like this bus.*

She took a deep breath. The thought used to unsettle her, but not today.

Viewed from the bus, last night doesn't seem real. She replays it in her mind, picturing her childhood bedroom with its single bed snug in one corner, the duvet washed into lumps by her mother and only partly confined by a faded cover missing most of its buttons. The room has an air of pungent sadness about it. The dim light of the fitting in the centre of the ceiling barely reaches the curtains hanging limply at the window like wind-weary flags on a still day. Next to the bed, her case lies open on the floor. Beside it, are piled the last things to be packed: a couple of guidebooks, a few framed photos she doesn't want to risk in the hold of the aircraft, sunglasses, a pack of work-related documents to read on the journey, and a last minute purchase – the new swimsuit in a brave shade of red.

She remembers going down on her knees by the suitcase, a rush of feelings rising like nausea inside her. Nerves? No. Excitement iced with fear. Naming the emotions helps her to deal with them and she finishes the packing calmly, tucking chargers and adaptors into corners, checking her list.

She straightens her back, her mobile phone rings.

'Hi Jenny! You packed?'

'Just about.'

'OK. I'll see you tomorrow at the station, in the car park like we said?'

'That's great, Anna, thanks.'

'What time do your parents get back?'

'Not till late.'

'OK, sleep well. I'd love to see their faces when they get home!'

As she puts the phone down on the floor beside her, Jenny feels a warm, purring presence rub up against her back. The cat pads round to face her, tail in the air, for all the world asking, 'Are you off again?'

'Oh Spock, you know what suitcases mean, don't you.' She rubs his head between his pointy ears. 'But it's not a trip back to uni this time. Come on, let's put you out for your night-time adventures, it'll be Mum doing this from now on.'

Getting up from the floor having closed the case, she catches sight of herself in the dressing table mirror. Her reflection stares back. No change there. Medium brown hair framing a slim face which has nothing wrong with it that she can see, but which never makes boys want to take a second look. Average height and weight, perfectly acceptable figure. Jenny wrinkles her nose and turns away. Because she never smiles when she sees her own reflection, she is unaware of the impact her smile has on those who are fortunate enough to see it, and who always remember her for it. As a teenager, her head turned by girls' magazines, she asked her parents what they thought her best feature was. Her mother found something nice to say, Jenny could no longer remember what. Her father said,

'You're no trouble, Jenny, I'll say that for you.'

Her parents had lived all their married lives in the same house on Headley Way. Now that they were retired, and

Jenny was past the stage of needing to be ferried up and down to university, they had sold their car. The bus was very convenient. It took them to the city centre for shopping and was handy for the JR if ever that were necessary, God forbid. The car was gone.

'It'll save us a bloody fortune,' said her father, and they all took the bus from then on.

In fact, Jenny loved to sit and observe the constantly changing world of the bus, the random collection of souls who became fellow passengers for a brief time. Occasionally they would chat, more often they would keep themselves to themselves; a very public privacy.

How often had she been on this route? It could be a metaphor for life. You journey from stop to stop, hook up with some people on the way, lose touch with others, as you travel to your destination. Sometimes that's not the one you expected, everyone knew that visitors and tourists regularly lost their way in Oxford, and she herself, born and brought up here, would never have expected to be going where she was headed now.

One of the generation of graduates to learn that an arts degree was no guarantee of a job, Jenny had found herself without an income. She had no choice but to ask if she could move back home, and her parents had no choice but to say yes. They were all disappointed. Her mother, who had never wanted more than to marry and have a family, nevertheless hoped that her only daughter would have a career. Apprenticed in a factory straight from school, her father had never seen the point of academic study, and she knew that they had struggled to help her financially during her student years.

Waitressing. That was the first job, the first stop on the journey. She registered with the local agencies, and was offered some contract catering work at the Said Business School, near the station. It was an easy commute on the bus so she jumped at it. It wasn't long before she caught the eye of the Events and Programme Manager who was looking for additional help during the conference season and didn't like paying agency rates for casual workers. Undergraduate staff were easy to find in the vacations, but didn't stay long. Graduates with initiative who would stick around were rarer. Jenny worked hard and related well to the business clients. She learned to recognise up-and-coming management types in the gym-taut younger men with jackets and open-necked shirts, no tie; an informality which permitted the use of first names.

'James Sawyer? Welcome, James, here's your information pack. You'll find coffee waiting for you over there.'

With the older men (suit, tie and a thicker waistline), formality and deference went down better.

'Good morning, Mr Beardsley! Let me find your name badge for you.'

Soon she was promoted to supervise the front of house team whose job it was to 'meet and greet' conference delegates, and this was how she met Dominic. He was booked in for a Global Leadership Conference organised by the international hotel chain he worked for. He had got caught up in the road works on the Oxford ring road, arrived very late and missed the welcome session. Open-necked white shirt, she noted when she saw him hurrying in. Jacket that looked made for him in a fine wool fabric, nice shoes – not particularly clean but expensive-looking. Having put him down as a no-show, she had gone out of her way to get him his badge and welcome pack personally, then helped him slip unobtrusively into the first session. He bought her a drink after hours to thank her and seemed very interested in her experience in the hospitality industry. Many weeks and several interviews later, here she was, several stops along the way, recruited onto their Fast-track Graduate Programme, and about to start a twelve-month trial in Guest Relations in the Middle East, where Dominic was to be Programme Manager for the launch of a new hotel. It was a region, he told her, where good service was of paramount importance. And where petrol was cheaper than water.

The sound of a car horn on St Aldate's brought her back to reality. Jenny felt her stomach clench again. To distract herself, she went over the day's schedule: the reassurance of the No 13 bus to the station where she would meet Anna, sassy, silky-haired Anna, the girl who had come up to talk to the shy little thing backed into the corner of the playground on their first day at secondary school. True, she had not gone along with Jenny's dream of going on the school trip to France, the cost was too high for both their families, but it was Anna who helped her write her personal statement for her university application, got drunk on vodka and coke with her when they were both offered places, and who had been hanging onto her other suitcase for the past few days. It was all planned: train from Oxford station to London; Heathrow Express to the airport; then the flight.

Flight. Was she running away from, or towards something? She had hoped that going over the arrangements one more time would calm her, but the jitters in her stomach were still there. Until she thought of her father. This time tomorrow, she would be on the other side of the world. What would he say then?

Jenny tried hard to maintain a professional composure when the door to her hotel room was thrown open.

'Your suitcases are coming, Miss Jennifer.'

The first wonderful thing she saw was a bed you could get lost in; dunes of tasselled cushions piled high on white cotton sheets with the crisp finish only professional laundering can give. Dominic had told her she would be put up in the hotel for a month to give her time to settle in and find an apartment. Jenny had not expected a sea view, even though it was low season, and wondered if his influence had anything to do with it. She explored the marble-lined bathroom and stroked the softness of the towels, which immediately made her think of Spock and look for another distraction. How did the experience rate so far? She wasn't here on holiday. Check-in had been efficient and courteous - nothing to make a note of there. The door buzzer signalled the arrival of her bags. Enough for today. Hanging up a few clothes for the morning, she abandoned her case and, still wondering at her surroundings, climbed into one side of the enormous bed and fell helplessly asleep.

Spears of sunlight shooting through a crack between the heavy curtains woke her. Her alarm had not gone off yet, it was still early. She stepped out of the air-conditioned chill of her room onto the balcony, listened to the waves spilling up the beach and breathed in the heavy, sea-scented air. The sky was a pure, unblemished blue. Down below her, amidst the brazen pink and red splashes of bougainvillea flowers trailing from earthenware pots, squadrons of birds were walking slowly about on the ground, all of them with their beaks held wide open. Why the silent scream? It wasn't long before she understood as the hot, moisture-laden air clogged her lungs. How could anybody breathe here? When her nightdress began to stick to her back, she turned and slid between the curtains to escape the fierce beat of the sun's energy and a humidity that she had never before experienced.

Two hours later she was ready for her first day at work. Downstairs, her driver stood by the car, ready to take her to the company office for her induction. He opened the rear door with a nod, but as she bent to lower herself into the back seat as elegantly as her heels and office skirt would allow, she felt a heavy hand on her head pushing her into the back of the car like something under-baked being shoved back in the oven. The door slammed shut behind her.

'It's as if I were a criminal!' she thought, too surprised to express her indignation. This driver, with his yellow, nicotine-stained fingers was the older of the two Dominic had said could be available to her. It had not started well. When she called his number the night before to arrange the pick-up, he had insisted on coming 20 minutes later than she wanted, and ignored her questions about the morning traffic. She had given in, but was now regretting it. The air in the car was dominated by a pineapple-shaped air freshener dangling from the rear view mirror, obviously intended to mask the strong smell of petrol and apple tobacco. The combined chemical cocktail made her sneeze. They had driven off before she realised that her seatbelt was nowhere to be seen; it seemed to have disappeared somewhere beneath the back seat. Jenny broke a nail trying to find it, fought back tears, and when they arrived at the office ten minutes late, she resolved on asking for young Sami to drive her tomorrow, even if he was less experienced.

'How do you say *please would you drive a bit more slowly*?' she asked Dominic when they met up during the break in the first day's welcome session. 'He didn't seem to understand English, or perhaps he was just ignoring me.'

'A two word command only. Definitely no *please* and no *thank you*.' Dominic handed her a coffee. 'I've got a list of useful phrases somewhere, I'll get someone to give you a copy. Don't worry, you'll soon get the hang of things.'

Jenny wasn't sure. Jenny nodded.

Six months went by, but without the passing seasons that colour the passage of the English year. On the journey to work every morning, the sun was always shining, the sky always blue. She had been told that sudden, disruptive rain could appear from time to time, flooding roads not equipped with drains, but she had seen none so far. She didn't miss it.

Jenny had seen less and less of Dominic, he was always busy and had been away on several business trips, but she had heard that he was back for the second quarter business review. He put his head round the office door.

'Hi Jenny, how's my protégée doing?'

He waited, already sure of the answer.

Jenny rolled her chair back from her desk, leaned back and crossed her legs, the office lights reflected in the patent sheen of her heeled court shoes. She had bought two scarily expensive pairs to boost her morale for the new job, one black (she kept neutrals for work, colour for her days off) and this pair, an equally versatile nude. Her mother would have called them beige. She smiled up at Dominic, ready to talk figures.

'You mean the business? As if you didn't know that the hotel occupancy rate is ahead of target!'

He leaned against the doorframe, nodding.

'And Food & Beverage sales are running at 37% over budget.' She gazed up at him but said nothing more. He grinned back at her and turned to leave the office. It was just as he had expected. Over his shoulder she heard,

'Awesome!'

And so it was. The brutal heat began to lessen, or perhaps Jenny just got used to it. Sami was a willing and cheerful driver, accepting her directions even when she got them wrong. She found herself an affordable flat with the tiniest of balconies so that she could enjoy the thought of opening the door and going outside, even if she never did, at least not until the 'winter' finally arrived and she could begin to risk the sun on her fair skin.

Work was going well: she had a sure instinct for hospitality and was willing to adapt to the local corporate bureaucracy. She sent long emails with reams of photos to her parents, knowing that her father would never look at them and her mother would show them to anyone who didn't think of an excuse fast enough. She used WhatsApp to stay in touch with her old friends, happy to hear them say how jealous they were of her tan. She felt like a local.

Almost 12 months in, it was already near the end of her trial appointment and the first chance to take any leave. She shopped for presents at the Souk and, embarrassed by the pleas of eager merchants, bought more than she had friends or relatives to give to. The flights were booked, her bags were packed. For the first time since she had left Oxford, she allowed herself to feel homesick.

'Hi, Jenny. Come in and sit down.' Dominic was looking pleased with himself. 'I've got a surprise for you before you go off on leave.'

'Sorry…?'

Dominic grinned and tossed her a fat, A4 envelope. 'Congratulations!'

Jenny just managed to catch the package. She frowned.

'What's this?'

'I think you'll find it's what you wanted. Go on, open it!'

She ran her thumb under the flap of the envelope and pulled out a formal-looking document in Arabic and English.

'You're a natural, and not having worked for any of the rival hotel chains, there were no bad habits for us to iron out.'

He was rewarded by one of those smiles.

'It's all there, no need to worry, you are sponsored for a full two-year contract, housing allowance, flight allowance, yearly paid leave including the local Feast days, a salary increase in line with your appointment as Guest Relations Assistant Manager, and look,' he pointed to a clause at the top of one page, 'You are even guaranteed a supply of *cold fresh drinking water*!'

Jenny looked. It was true.

That was when she knew she had cracked it.

Dominic took it quite well really, she reflected, after he had calmed down. Of course, first there was the anger, the attempts to dissuade her and, surprisingly, his evident disappointment. She hadn't expected that, but she didn't doubt he would find another candidate soon enough, so she stood her ground on her high heels and finally convinced him. She wanted to apply for a transfer back to one of the hotels in the UK. He recognised the signs, ultimately accepted her choice, and agreed to pass her request back to head office, even adding his commendation.

Eventually, Jenny was back on the bus, settled into her usual seat with her case by her side, forehead pressed against the smooth glass of the window. The No 13 hummed off on its routine trawl backwards and forwards between the station and the JR, gathering up passengers at one stop, relinquishing them at another.

I'm a creature of habit, she thought as she watched the familiar street scenes shifting past. *Just like this bus.*

She took a deep breath. What would they say when they heard her news? She waited as the stone of the city centre gave way to the brick and render of residential housing.

Soon be home.

oxford

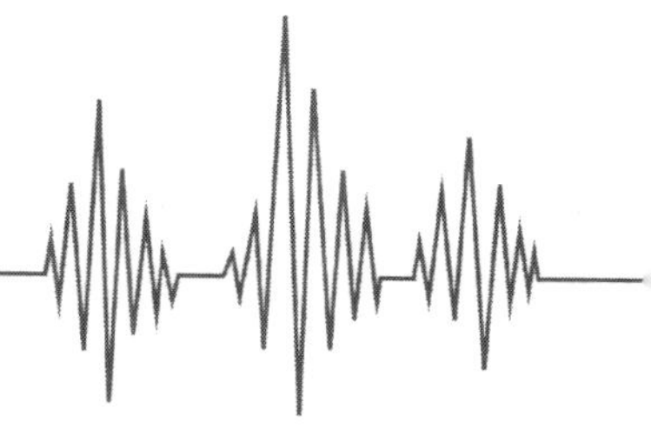

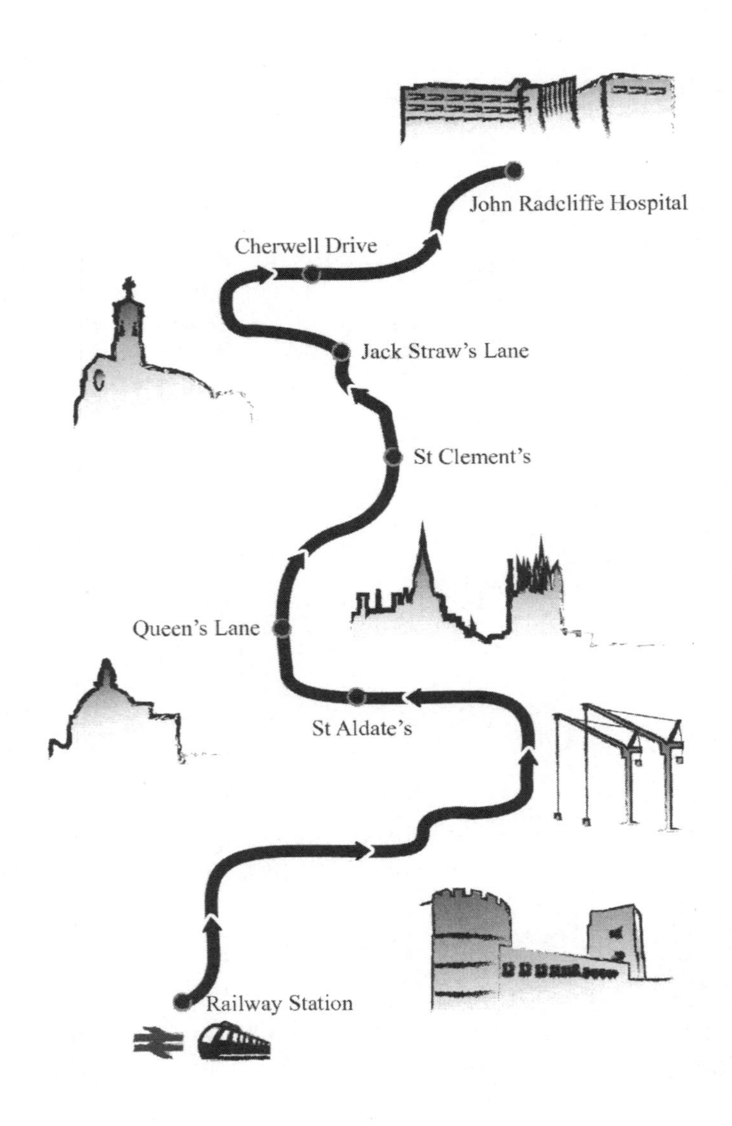
John Radcliffe Hospital
Cherwell Drive
Jack Straw's Lane
St Clement's
Queen's Lane
St Aldate's
Railway Station

Everything I Do

SARAH TIPPER

In the timetable of my life, is marriage running late? Dennis, the bus driver, wondered. He stopped on St Aldate's, took on some passengers then had a few moments to wait before pulling off into the unrelenting traffic again. He thought of his girlfriend Gemma. She would be eating her cheese and pickle sandwich about now, having her break in the staff room of the book shop she worked in. He looked over the road at the iron gates and remembered when they were young and broke. Going for walks in Christ Church Meadow was one of their favourite things to do in those early days. It was free and all that had mattered was being together, in private, able to say whatever they needed to say as they tried out this new scary thing of interest in the opposite sex. Gemma always had strawberry bonbons in her handbag. He smiled at the memory of the taste and the dusting of pink powdered sugar, transferred from her lips to his and then back again. Delicious. Like pollen that germinated their teenage love into something sturdier, something like the horse chestnut tree they once sheltered under from the rain.

It was helping the woman in pink on to the bus at the train station that had made him think of weddings, although he'd been thinking about the close cousins of the wedding; the proposal and the engagement, with increasing frequency recently. He glanced back at the pinkness in his mirror. She was chatting to the sprightly old fella who often got the bus this time of day. Of course you could get married on a weekday lunchtime now, with a minimum of fuss if you wanted, just close family and friends in the Register Office. It didn't have to be on a Saturday and a source of stress and big spending.

Dennis left the St Aldate's bus stop. He saw a driver he knew and waved. Both of them were driving buses as red as a post box, but were transporting people not letters. People full of potential words versus paper full of captured, fixed words. Sometimes people had trouble getting their words out, paper and pen could help. The post boxes outside the Post Office opposite the Town Hall were the only ones Dennis had ever seen made of wood rather than the traditional red metal. Gemma said she'd seen a gold post box at the top of Divinity Road. From gold post boxes his thoughts travelled to gold rings. Maybe he should propose in a letter, she wouldn't expect it, and that would get his words out. Dennis had applied to be a postman at the same time as he applied to be a bus driver. The bus company had replied first and so here he was. Well, he was also all over town, Headington and Abingdon in the course of his working day. His best friend Dave was a postman. Both of them covered a lot of miles. At least bus driving was indoors thought Dennis. Both jobs needed a strong bladder. Dave claimed his was trained by years of sinking pints. Dennis rarely drank alcohol, it wasn't compatible with his job. Gemma teased him when he got squiffy on their all-inclusive holiday and called him a cheap date. When Dennis had a drink nowadays it was always because of a special occasion. You've got to have a drink at a wedding, toasting fizzily to the future.

Dave said being married was a doddle. He'd be the obvious choice for best man, if Dennis were to get married. Gemma liked Dave. Good old Dave. Dave had proposed to Tracy ten years ago with a hand painted sign scrawled on an old bedsheet attached to the first roundabout Tracy passed on her drive to work. The day that Dave had hung the bed sheet Tracy had gone the other way to work, needing to pop in on her Mum to lend her a can of hairspray. Tracy had come home from work unaware she'd been proposed to. Dave had made her get back in the car. She had resisted, saying she was tired, but he had insisted. They had driven round the roundabout three times then gone home where Dave knelt on the kerb and asked in words rather than via a bedsheet if Tracy would marry him and Tracy said yes. Dave liked to say his Mother-in-law had nearly prevented their union by having big hair. Dave's brother had made a joke about it in the best man speech. That was a proposal with a story to it, how could Dennis top that?

Of course Phil would have something to say about it if Dennis were to ask Gemma to make an honest man of him. 'Make an honest man of him' was a horrible phrase thought Dennis, resolving never to use it out loud. It was outdated, like living in sin. When Dave got married Phil had made a joke about having lost Dave in a terrible accident when his finger became trapped in a wedding ring. Dave said Phil was just jealous because he wasn't getting any. Then Phil said he did alright thank you very much, then Dave stroked his chin in an exaggerated fashion reminiscent of the school yard and said 'Jimmy Hill' (in their school boy way of casting doubt upon the veracity of the speaker's claims) and Dennis changed the subject.

Gemma didn't think much of Phil. She said he was weird and always had been. Dennis privately agreed but publicly defended his other best mate from school. Phil had dropped out of a Philosophy degree and he wanted big talk on days like wedding days when small talk was more suitable and expected. Lucky weather, bride lovely, bridesmaids' dresses a pleasant colour, food superb, that's all you need words-wise at a wedding.

Phil often asked Dennis how he kept from going mad, driving around in circles all day. Phil also said life's a journey, not a destination, unless you're a bus driver. Dennis wasn't sure what Phil meant by that. He wasn't sure that Phil knew either. Dennis had once explained to Phil that a hive mind sat behind him. On a wet Monday morning he could feel the gloom, on a bright Friday afternoon with a bus full of schoolkids he could feel (and hear) the excitement. On a Saturday early evening he saw well-groomed hopeful people at their best, on a Saturday late evening he saw masks slip, hands on knees, smudged make-up and sometimes felt a chill descend and eyes averted, as voices were raised in anger. The bus had a mood to it, the enclosed community existed from stop to stop, being made, unmade and re-made constantly. Dennis wasn't going round in circles, it was different every time. Just one passenger could alter the mood; a cheerful toddler, a drunk, a loud and indiscreet phone call, all could cause smiles or frowns.

Dennis nearly said that at least he had a useful job when Phil started going on about sociological studies of bus drivers and their poor occupational health. Phil was a lazy arse, plain and simple. He'd had many short term jobs but nothing stuck. Phil had done better than Dennis or Dave at school but in the words of their headmaster 'He could never apply himself properly'.

Dennis frowned about how the work shirts that Gemma ironed for him had got larger over the years. He thought about Phil asking Dave what he wanted to get married for and knew he'd be asked the same question. He knew Phil would scoff at Gemma's little notes in his packed lunch. She always told him to drive safely and not let grumpy people get him down. She always cheered him up on days when everyone had wanted to pay their fare with a twenty pound note.

The woman in pink got off and Dennis wondered about the events leading up to the wedding she was attending. Even when you'd decided to propose and you were sure of a good response, how did you do it? How? Dennis realised he'd decided he was going to. It wasn't if that concerned him, it was how.

Dennis almost always thought of Gemma at this bus stop. It was near what used to be Milham Ford girl's school, the school she'd been at when they met. He was an Oxford Boys boy, along with Dave and Phil. He'd met her at a discreet distance from school and they'd gone to the pictures to see *Robin Hood Prince of Thieves*. Sometimes he sang the Bryan Adams theme tune 'Everything I Do (I Do It For You)' to her and she called him a soppy sod.

He was fitter then of course. He glanced down at his middle, plump like a cushion. People went on diets before they got married. Would Gemma start fretting more about the half a stone she always wanted to lose? Maybe in future teleporters would be invented and he could stop being a bus driver and be something else, something that would give him the body of an Adonis. Beam me up Scotty! Maybe there would be driverless buses, but he didn't think so, a bus can't think for itself, it can't predict some of the mad things Oxford cyclists do.

While Dennis sat at the JR waiting to begin the next leg of his journey it came to him that Christ Church Meadows would be the perfect place to propose. He would get some batteries for his old ghetto blaster and have Bryan Adams playing while he gave her a ring hidden inside a bag of strawberry bonbons. Dennis smiled as he planned to visit the sweet shop when he finished his shift on the High Street.

oxford

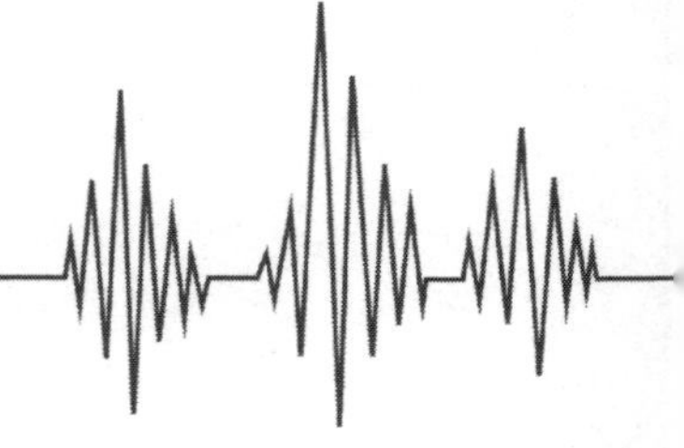